HER OWN DEVICES

A steampunk adventure novel
Magnificent Devices Book Two

Shelley Adina

Moonshell
Books

Moonshell Books, Inc.
www.moonshellbooks.com

Book Layout ©2013 BookDesignTemplates.com
Art by Claudia McKinney at phatpuppyart.com
Images from Shutterstock.com, used under license
Design by Kalen O'Donnell
Author font by Anthony Piraino at OneButtonMouse.com

Her Own Devices / Shelley Adina — 2nd ed.
ISBN 978-1-939087-09-6

For my readers,
who clamored for more about the Lady

1

London, August 1889

They were too small to be airships, and too ephemeral to be bombs. Glowing with a gentle orange light, each the size of a lantern, they floated up into the night sky powered by a single candle and the most delicate of tiny engines.

One didn't, after all, simply release such dangerous things without a means of directing where they were to go.

"They're so pretty," Maggie breathed.

"Sh!" Her twin sister Lizzie, both of them having no surname that anyone knew, nudged her with urgency. "The Lady said to be quiet."

"You be quiet! Since when d'you listen to the Lady at the best o' times?"

"Mopsies!" Lady Claire Trevelyan, sister of a viscount, formerly a resident of Belgravia and now a resident of a hideout in Vauxhall gained at the price of a brigand's life, glared at both girls. They'd been on many a night lookout. What were they thinking, to risk giving away their position by whispering?

Though Claire had to admit that the beauty of the balloons' dreamy flight hid the fact that she, Jake, and Tigg had constructed them out of a rag picker's findings: a silk chemise, a ragged nightgown so fine she could draw it through her grandmother's emerald ring, a pair of bloomers that a very broad lady had thrown away because of a tear she was too wealthy to mend.

Add to this a little device Claire had been working on that would act as a steering and propulsion mechanism, and you had a set of silent intruders that could go where she and her accomplices could not.

Hunching their shoulders at the reproof, the girls settled behind the tumbledown remains of a churchyard wall to watch the half-dozen balloons sail away with their cargo over the width of a street and up over a two-story stone wall as impregnable as a medieval keep.

The spider takes hold with her hands, and is in kings' palaces. Well, tonight she was the spider and the inhabitants of "The Cudgel" Bonaventure's fortress were about to learn a lesson in manners. One did not jump the associates of the Lady in the street and relieve them of the rewards of their night's work in the gambling parlors without reprisal. The candles that caused the balloons to rise would not set his fortress on fire, but the chemical suspended in a single vial from each certainly would.

An owl hooted, rather more cheerfully than one might expect. "They're over the wall," Snouts McTavish translated. "We can move in when you give the word, Lady."

"I think it will be safe to wait for Mr. Bonaventure in the street. Jake, do you have the gaseous capsaicin devices should he prove foolish?"

"Aye."

She had known Jake for several weeks. Even now, she was not sure he wouldn't use such a device on her and challenge Snouts for lieutenancy of their little band of the abandoned and neglected. However, if someone were to prove himself trustworthy, he must perforce be trusted. Leaving him in charge of the satchel with its clinking contents was a calculated risk, but it was one she must take. Especially since he had compounded the devices himself.

"Right, then. Let us offer advice to the distressed and homeless, shall we?"

The glow over the wall was bright enough to light their way into the street as the buildings behind it caught fire. The contents of each vial suspended beneath its balloon had ignited on contact with air as the candles burned out and they dropped out of flight, higgledy-piggledy all over the roof of The Cudgel's headquarters. Wood that had been dried out during the hot summer—old wood, that had been standing since long before their glorious Queen's time—ignited and in seconds the oldest part of the building had gone up like a Roman candle.

Claire regretted the loss of the steering mechanisms—a particularly nice bit of engineering she was quite proud of—but at least they had gone in a good cause.

The Cudgel would think twice before picking on her friends again.

The entire house was engulfed in roaring flame by the time the single gate creaked open and a small crowd of men and boys tumbled through it, gasping and slapping smoldering sparks and holding bits of clothing over their faces against the smoke.

Hmph. And where were the women holding positions in The Cudgel's hierarchy? Her opinion of his leadership dropped even lower.

The wailing of the fire engines in the distance told her she must be succinct.

"Mr. Bonaventure!" she called, stepping into full view in the middle of the street. She had dressed carefully in raiding rig for the occasion, in a practical black skirt that could be rucked up by means of internal tapes should she have to run or climb. She had dispensed with a hat for the evening, choosing instead to simply leave her driving goggles sitting in front of her piled hair, a gauzy scarf wound over it and around her neck. A leather corselet contained a number of hooks and clasps for equipment, and instead of her trusty rucksack, which Jake was wearing, she now wore a leather harness with a spine holster specially made to the contours of the lightning rifle she had taken from Lightning Luke

Jackson three weeks ago. She was pleased to see that her lacy blouse remained pristine white, despite the half-hour spent huddled behind the wall.

She slid the rifle from its holster over her shoulder and held it loosely, her index finger hovering over the power switch.

In ones and twos, the small crowd of smoked criminals realized what she held—and therefore, who she was. Slowly, they backed against the wall, leaving The Cudgel exposed to her aim.

Hmph. So much for honor among thieves.

The Cudgel eyed her. "I know you. Wot business you got 'ere?"

The sirens sounded closer. They would be crossing the Southwark Bridge over the Thames even now. "Just this," she said, enunciating crisply so that there would be no misunderstanding. "Last night your men set upon four of my friends returning from the gaming halls, and took everything they had. This is a warning to you that I do not tolerate abuse of my friends or the fruit of their honest labor."

"Izzat so," he drawled. "Can't say as I know wot yer babbling on."

She hefted the rifle and pushed the power switch. "I suggest you apply your limited intellect to it."

His head thrust forward like that of an angry bulldog whose bone has just been ripped from its teeth. "I say you go back to your needlepoint like a good little girl and think about wot I'm goin' to do to you for—"

The gun hummed happily, its pitch and frequency announcing that it was ready for work. Claire's index finger now rested on the trigger.

"If I hear that you have stepped foot in Vauxhall, with or without evil intent, your own yellow belly will be the last thing you ever see."

Yellow belly? Goodness. That was a line straight out of one of the melodramatic flickers she and Emilie had been addicted to centuries ago—two months ago—when she had been a green girl.

"I'd say you owe me, then, girlie—"

"You may address me as the Lady."

He started across the street. "And you must address this. Creeper! Hiram! Hold her down." He fumbled with the buttons on his trousers, while Claire stared in astonishment. Really. With the fire engines nearly upon them and his house burning to cinders as they spoke, he thought he could threaten her by means of his disgusting person?

Creeper and Hiram, whoever they were, did not, in fact, hold her down. However, two shadows detached from the main body of the huddle and slipped away down the alley at the corner of the wall. Snouts, Jake, and Tigg formed an immovable mass at her back.

Claire sighed. "Really, Mr. Bonaventure. You should not, as my mother often told me, use a pin when a needle is called for. Particularly so dull and short a pin."

She pulled the trigger and a bolt of lightning shot across the street, singeing him neatly between the legs and burning the inner seams of his canvas trousers clean away.

The Cudgel screamed and leaped back six feet, the scent of burning flesh overlaid on the smoke that filled the air. Hysterical, no doubt in pain at least equal to that he had hoped to inflict upon her, he capered and screeched so that Claire could hardly distinguish between him and the sirens of the engines as they roared up the cobbled street.

"Billy Bolt!" With the signal to scatter, her friends slipped into the shadows with her before anyone in authority could say they'd been there.

Snouts waited until they were nearly back in their own neighborhood before he said, "Been gettin' a little target practice in, I see. It'll look like 'e got burnt by the fire and none o' that lot will say different."

"I have indeed." The furthest corner of the garden wall was scorched and pockmarked as proof. "There is no point in being considered armed and dangerous if one cannot actually hit anything."

"Lucky that gun is accurate."

"It's more than accurate, Snouts. You've seen yourself how it practically feels your aim. Even Willie could hit a target with it, I'm sure."

"Lady, please tell me you ent gonna—"

"No, certainly not. No one touches this rifle but me … or you, when you are acting in my stead. It's more than just a weapon, you know. It stands for what we've accomplished."

Snouts said no more, just kept pace with her, one eye on the others to make sure no one fell behind and no one was in pursuit, and the other on the street ahead, watching for danger.

Claire was the first to admit that keeping order in a band of thieves and cutpurses would be nearly impossible without the rifle—or rather, without their belief in what she might do with it. The truth was, she had only fired it outside the garden three times: Twice on the night it had come into her possession, and tonight.

Clearly she had inherited not only her father's aptitude for firearms, but also his belief that one did not need to speak much, only to say what was worth hearing when one did. Or, as Polgarth the poultryman at the family pile in Cornwall was wont to say, Walk soft an' carry a big stick.

She was thankful that at least Snouts, Tigg, and the Mopsies followed her lead without coercion. Since she had lost her home in the Arabian Bubble riots and fallen in with this street gang that was no more than a rabble of desperate, hungry children, they had taught her how to survive—and she had taught them how to thrive.

Between lessons in reading and mathematics, they rehearsed new and confounding hands of Cowboy Poker, the current rage they had fabricated in the drawing rooms and gambling halls of London. Those with a bent for chemistry and mechanics assisted her in the assembly of her devices. Food appeared on the table with heartening regularity now, and they all had more than one suit of clothes each. Even Rosie, the hen she had rescued, who ruled the desolate garden behind the cottage with an iron claw, had begun to put on weight.

And to top it all, tomorrow she was to begin employment as assistant to Andrew Malvern, M.Sc., Royal Society of Engineers.

The watchman on the roof platform above the river

entrance whistled, and Snouts whistled three notes in return. The door swung open, allowing a wide bar of warm light to spill onto the planks that had been repaired after a series of unfortunate explosions caused by the previous inhabitants.

"Lady! You're back. What happened?" Lewis asked eagerly before he was fairly through the door.

Weepin' Willie, a mute boy of five, pushed through the legs of the boys crowding the porch, and flung himself into Claire's arms. She hugged him, a warm rush of gratitude spilling through her that here, at least, was one person in all the world who loved her without reservation. The others respected her, perhaps even liked her. But this small scrap of humanity had stuck to her like a burr from the moment she'd met him. Because of him—well, because of them all, really, she'd kept to her course and not gone down to Cornwall beaten and defeated, to be the bride of some country squire chosen by her mother.

"The Cudgel will not be waylaying any of you in the future," she told them, setting Willie on his feet and getting up. "He has a permanent reminder to mind his manners henceforth."

Snouts made a gesture in the vicinity of his pants that caused the boys' eyes to widen in horror and admiration.

She was committed to her new life now, for good or ill.

Of course, The Cudgel aside, avoiding ill was at the top of her list of priorities. For that reason, she had allowed her new employer to believe she was the governess of five of these children, and part of their agreement was that they might supplement their education in his laboratory on occasion.

Surely she would be able to keep her secret. After all, he had not inquired too closely about her place of residence or who, exactly, would allow their children out with her to perform experiments in a riverside warehouse. She would just have to remain pleasantly vague about certain details, and trust that his natural reserve and politeness would prevail.

It would never do for him to know that he was harboring the infamous Lady of Devices, inadvertent murderer of Lightning Luke Jackson and reigning queen of the south side underworld.

Her reputation in society would never recover.

2

"Miss, a word, if you please." Granny Protheroe, who was their cook and possessed some tenuous relationship to Lewis that had never been satisfactorily explained, stepped outside into the walled garden where the Mopsies were attempting to encourage some beans and peas to grow. She gazed at the brave trellises made of string with narrow-eyed pessimism. "That hen'll eat them things before they're an inch taller. Besides, it's too late in the summer to grow such."

Claire watched the girls, who labored on as if they had not heard. "Perhaps they might surprise you. Rosie is more fond of things with legs than things with leaves." She turned to Granny. "What would you like to speak about?"

"That hen don't produce enough eggs, and it's silly to barter for 'em. We oughter have a flock."

The Mopsies came to instant attention. "A flock? More hens like Rosie?"

Maggie ran to them and took Claire's hand. "Please, Lady, c'n we 'ave 'em? Rosie needs a flock. She must be lonely out 'ere."

Rosie showed no signs whatever of loneliness. Quite the opposite—a feathered despot, she had quite cowed poor Lewis and some of the smaller boys, who wouldn't go in the garden no matter what the provocation. Claire gathered her arguments.

"My dear girls, if we did such a thing and came under attack by The Cudgel or his like, who would protect these hens?"

"We would, same as we protect Rosie now." Lizzie glared, as if Claire had impugned her ability to take care of her own. "It was us as saved 'er in the first place, innit?"

"Yes, but it is much easier to fight or flee with a single bird. How would you make for safety if you had four? Six?"

"We could have six?" Maggie's face lit up.

"I was using a hypothetical number."

"Wot's hyp—hypofet—"

"Imaginary. For instance."

"Oh. Well, 'at's simple. We wouldn't run. The rifle'd put paid to anyone 'oo comes round."

"We can't depend on the rifle for everything," Claire pointed out. "The sad example of Lightning Luke has shown us that."

"We make 'em a house," Lizzie said. "One that moves, so we c'n take 'em wiv us."

"Or floats," Maggie put in. "They could sleep on the river and come up into the garden in the mornings."

"We're not talking about ducks," Granny Protheroe informed them. "Hens don't like water. Ent you ever heard of 'madder'n a wet hen'? Besides, they'd be stolen by some waterbug, like as not, and et. How'd you like that?"

Maggie's eyes filled with tears, and Claire hastened to say, "It is a fine idea, though. A moveable coop. Would you put it on treads, like a steambus, or legs, like those automatons we saw at the Crystal Palace?"

"Legs," the twins said in unison.

Claire tried not to show her glee at finally hitting on a project for this stubborn pair that would combine all the best lessons she could teach—a project they were motivated to do out of feminine protective instincts, the strongest on earth.

"Excellent," she said. "We will begin with drawings— " Art and perspective. "—and proceed to building the structure." Mathematics and physics. "We will need a small steam engine to power it, and some means by which to operate the legs." Mechanics.

"When can we get the hens?"

Claire sighed. One thing at a time. "As you make your way through the city tomorrow, you must keep your eyes open. I have no doubt that Rosie was not the only chicken in London in need of rescuing. But no stealing, mind. The birds you find must be in honest need of a home."

"Why are we going into the city?" Lizzie wanted to know. "We ought t'stay on this side of the river and lie low after last night."

"It is my first day as Mr. Malvern's assistant, so I can drive you as far as Blackfriars. Snouts will take you on a reconnaissance mission to gather materials for your coop. You might have some success in the scrap-yards behind the foundries. We will work on a list later to-day." Measurements and penmanship.

The hens won out over Lizzie's natural caution. She and her sister turned back to the pea trellis, chattering in low voices about what the walking coop should look like. Granny Protheroe had gone back inside, leaving Claire to pace the length of the garden alone. *Garden* was a grandiose word for the half-acre riot of brambles and potholes blasted out of the earth, all enclosed in a six-foot wall at least a foot thick. No toll-taker needed such a wall; only the criminals who had appropriated the tumbledown cottage would in order to defend their territory. Had Lightning Luke used the ground for tar-get practice of some kind? A missile or an explosive might gouge holes like these.

Not that they bothered Rosie in the least. Claire watched the red hen throwing dirt in the air with aban-don as she enjoyed a dust bath at the bottom of a small crater. "I'm glad you're finding these useful," she said. "I trust you're prepared to share. The Mopsies will be bringing some companions for you soon."

Rosie blinked in slow contentment, utterly uncon-cerned about the prospect of rivals.

"I wish I had your *sangfroid*." The truth was, she

was a little nervous about beginning work at the laboratory. Doubts and fears swarmed her confidence like mosquitoes. Would Lord James Selwyn be there? Would he find some way to sabotage her efforts and make her look incompetent? He had been in a barely concealed rage the last time she'd seen him. Had that temper burned itself out, or was it merely banked until the next confrontation?

The memory of his attempt to bribe her into turning down Andrew Malvern's offer of employment had been both infuriating and mortifying. Even now, the thought of his insolence at the Crystal Palace made her cheeks burn and her blood run hot.

Yes, it was true that taking his money would have turned all her dreams of a university degree and a career into reality. But at what cost?

Her own integrity, that's what.

The children's safety.

And Mr. Malvern's regard.

She could not afford to lose the first or second, and as for the third ... well, he was to be her employer, wasn't he? Of course she wanted his good opinion.

As would any reasonable person.

Snouts, the Mopsies, and Weepin' Willie—who could not be persuaded to stay at home helping Granny Protheroe to make pies, if there were more birds like his adored Rosie to be found—joined the crowd swarming across the Blackfriars bridge.

"You're sure you don't want to go with them?" Claire watched the little group as long as she could, but they were soon lost to sight.

Tigg shifted in the seat beside her. "I'll go if you say to, Lady, but I druther stick by you." His voice dropped to a mumble. "Might learn summat useful."

The warmth of approval colored her tone as she said quietly, "I have no doubt you will, and I applaud your determination to get on, Tigg." Smiling, Claire steered the steam landau down the warren of narrow streets until she reached Orpington Close—another grandiose name for a lane to the river barely wide enough to admit her and her gleaming engine. "I am quite sure Mr. Malvern could use a tender for his experiments with coal. And if he doesn't, we shall persuade him that at the very least, he must have someone to sweep up afterward. I certainly have no intention of wearing my duster while I work for fear of ruining my clothes."

She parked the landau and threw the switch that would shut down the flame and begin the boiler's cooling process, then climbed out. No coach bearing a noble crest stood there, or any other kind of vehicle, but Lord James could have come by hansom cab.

"Oh, stop," she muttered, unwinding her chiffon scarf and removing her driving goggles. "You have a perfect right to be here, and he can just take it like a gentleman."

"What's 'at, Lady?"

"Nothing, Tigg. Can you make sure the hood is secure, please? We don't want anyone being nosy while we're inside."

HER OWN DEVICES

Her duster over one arm, her navy skirt spotless and her hat in place, she waited by the door for him to check the latches on the brass hood flap that he kept polished to a gleam. He nodded in satisfaction and the two of them mounted the stairs to the loft, where Andrew Malvern kept his offices. The expanse below was filled with piles of building materials and an enormous glass chamber with brass rivets and hoses snaking in and out of it. Her back felt strangely naked without the weight of the lightning rifle, but even in this neighborhood, eyebrows might be raised if one arrived at the office armed.

No one need know it was under the seat of the landau.

Her employer raised his head as she reached the top of the stairs, and dropped his drafting pencil. "Miss Trevelyan! Er, I mean, Lady Claire. Good morning. I'm pleased to see you value punctuali—" He stopped halfway across the room. "Why, Tigg. I wasn't expecting you."

Tigg flushed with pleasure at being remembered. It had only been a week, but still ... many would consider a boy of thirteen beneath their notice.

Claire shook hands, and was close to coloring with pleasure herself when Andrew shook Tigg's as well, as though he were an equal. "I hope you do not mind his accompanying me. As you know, he has a talent for mechanics, and you did say that on occasion—"

"I did say so, and I meant it."

"If I can't help ye wi' that great engine downstairs, sir, I'll sweep ... or run errands ... or ..." Tigg struggled to control his emotions. "Appreciate it, sir," he finally mumbled.

"Your appearance is providential," Andrew confided. "It will speed my work enormously to have someone to work the coal tender while I conduct the experiments in the main chamber. I'm forever having to go back there and shovel coal into the hopper."

"I'm your man, sir." Tigg stood straighter.

"Excellent. You might go down and find an apron and one of the heavier pairs of gloves. If I am only to have you in the mornings, I shall make good use of you. I'll give Lady Claire some brief instructions, and we will begin immediately."

Tigg vanished down the stairs so quickly Claire wondered if his feet touched them at all.

"Thank you," she said softly. "He's been a different boy since we all met at the Crystal Palace and you showed him the workings of those engines."

"I admire an inquiring mind," Andrew said. "Tell me, has he had your landau into pieces yet?"

"Just the boiler. I'm afraid to let him touch the drive mechanisms to the wheels in case they don't go back together again. If worst comes to worst, at least I know how to reassemble the boiler."

Andrew laughed. "It's only a matter of time. Have I told you how pleased I am that you accepted my offer?"

"Not this morning."

"I should make it a daily practice."

"I trust Lord James has resigned himself to a better opinion of me, now that we will be working together?" She hardly dared hope that was so, but she had to know.

"I don't know, to be honest. The day after our fortuitous meeting at the Exhibition, he left for the Midlands to meet with the president of one of the railroads there." A shadow fell across his hazel eyes. "I wish he would wait until we had reliable results in hand, but what do I know? He is the man with the vision and the money. I'm just the man who puts it into practice. Glad-handing bankers and railroad presidents would give me hives, so it's fortunate he has a talent for it."

Claire's eyebrows rose at this unexpected confidence. Should he be telling her such things about his business? Then again, in the course of filing the stacks of paper teetering all around her, she would learn all about it whether he told her or not.

"Now." He gazed around the loft as though he wondered how all the mess had got there. "I believe you mentioned you had a plan when you were here for the interview?"

The disastrous interview, where she learned to her horror that Lord James had been prepared to court her—until he found out she was penniless and actually seeking employment with his partner—still burned in her memory. He had been so insulting she had fled.

Well, she was not prepared to flee now. No matter what he said, she would stand her ground and fight for what she wanted—which was to learn so much from Andrew Malvern that she could apply to The University of London to study engineering, and secure a letter of reference from him when the time came.

She dragged her attention from dreams of the future to the reality of the present. "Yes, I believe I said I would work in concentric circles, starting with the desk and moving outward."

"I have no filing system," he said meekly. "I trust you will institute one."

She had never done such a thing in her life. "Of course. I will use the method that seems most logical." She made it sound as if she had all the methods ever invented right at her fingertips, and he looked relieved.

"Right, then. I'll leave you to get started. At midday I'll take you and Tigg to lunch. We should celebrate your first day somehow." He smiled, and she lost her iron grip on her mental to-do list.

Claire gathered her wits as he rattled down the staircase, and focused on the desk. Never mind the fact that he was continually throwing her off balance. She had work to do.

By midday, she had managed to clear the desk, leaving only the drawings he had been working on, an inkwell, his pens and blotter, and a heavy book he seemed to be referencing in the drawing project. She had made her way through the stacks of journals, academic papers, receipts, and reports, pausing now and then to read a particularly interesting one. He had been sitting on a newspaper, so she fished it off the chair and shook it out, ready to use it to wrap parcels or start a fire in the potbellied stove. As she folded it, an advertisement with a portrait on the back page caught her eye.

HAVE YOU SEEN THIS YOUNG LADY?
PLEASE WRITE W/DETAILS
C/O THE EVENING STANDARD

"Good heavens!" Claire flung the paper at the stove in a kind of convulsion, then recovered herself and snatched it up again.

Took it over to the round, curtainless window, where there was more light.

It had to be a mistake.

The portrait, taken from the senior class daguerreotype and reproduced in the *Standard*'s line-drawing-ink-blot style, was of her.

3

By the time Andrew and Tigg came up to fetch her, the *Standard* had burned to ash in the bottom of the stove and Claire was industriously wiping the inkwell with a clean rag.

This is what you get for not answering your mother's letter, she told herself furiously as she ignited the landau and waited for Andrew to fold himself into the passenger seat and Tigg to climb into the small space behind them where the articulated brass top of the landau ratcheted down on fine days. *She is reduced to advertising for informants.*

As soon as they got back to the cottage, she would write a firmly worded letter to Cornwall. This nonsense must stop. With her luck, Julia Wellesley would see the

advertisement and turn it into the joke of the season—
because of course, anyone who must make their living
by default must have fallen off the social map.

"Will you direct me, sir?" She backed the landau
around until its forward lamps pointed up Orpington
Close, and released the lever that allowed the head of
steam to move them forward.

"Ladies' choice. What do you like?"

She liked a number of places—every single one of
which would be swarming with people she knew who
also read the *Evening Standard.*

Then again, what better way to spike the guns of
gossip than to appear as if everything were normal and
laugh it off as a curiosity? The drawing, after all, was
not that good a likeness.

"I should love to go to the Swan and Compass, in
Piccadilly. It's favored by the Churchill set, you know."
She steered for the bridge, and pushed the lever out to
the point that Andrew had to hang onto his hat.

"I say, what speed are we doing?"

"Thirty miles per hour."

He exchanged a huge grin with Tigg over his shoulder. "Marvelous. I never thought I'd see the day."

"It's a new day, Mr. Malvern," she said cheerfully as
they gained the bridge. Fortunately there were not too
many people or vehicles on it, though up ahead the traffic had slowed considerably as a dray backed into the
street.

Once they were past it and on the Victoria Embankment, she slowed to a respectable pace. "Are you
interested in learning to drive, sir?" she asked.

"You might well ask me if I'm interested in taking the transcontinental airship to South America and exploring the jungles." He still gripped his hat, though they were hardly going fast enough to stir up a breeze. "Both entail laying out vast sums and risking one's life."

"No risk in an airship," Tigg put in. "Safe as houses, I've 'eard. Not that I was ever in one. Closest I've been is seein' 'em go over."

"I was referring to the jungles. You are quite correct that airships are the safest and most efficient means of long-distance travel yet invented. But in answer to your question, Lady Claire, no, I have no desire to learn to drive. I have enormous admiration for those who do, however."

He slanted a glance at her that she was forced to ignore, or drive right over some unsuspecting pedestrian. Goodness. It almost sounded as though he admired her. But that could not be so. He had hired her for her mind.

Which was just as it should be.

"Here we are." She slowed to a stop half a block from the Swan and Compass, and by the time they reached the restaurant, she had regained her composure. He was only being kind. She must take people at their word, and stop reading personal meaning into casual conversation.

They were shown to a bright table in the window at the front, where they could watch people strolling to and fro on the sidewalk, and Claire saw Tigg watching carefully as Andrew pulled out a chair and seated her.

HER OWN DEVICES

With such an example, it wouldn't be long before the boy would be absorbing more than chemical formulas and theories of physics. With the opportunities the world offered in this modern age, he would not be forced to remain in the sphere in which she had found him. They might make a gentleman of him yet.

A lady enjoying lunch in a restaurant, she had been taught, might nibble delicately on a bit of endive, and sip tea with a pastry. But Claire was ravenous, and her mother was at the other end of the country. She ordered steak and mushroom pie with a salad, and devoured it so quickly and neatly that even Lady St. Ives might have wondered if it was ever actually there.

"I like to see a good appetite," Andrew observed, cutting up the last of his Dover sole. "My mother never could understand why it was necessary for titled young ladies to eat their dinners before they went out, so that it wouldn't look as though they were actually hungry."

"Was your mother taught that by her mother?"

"Oh, no. Mama was a cook in the Dunsmuir house. She had to send the young ladies' dinners up in the evening before they went out. She used to say at least she knew the girls enjoyed something they ate that evening."

"The girls?" Surely his mother had not been employed in the house of *those* Dunsmuirs. Do you mean the sisters of the boy who was ... "

"The very ones."

Tigg was looking from Claire to Andrew, clearly lost. "Wot boy? Wot 'appened to 'im?"

"You never heard the story?" Andrew refilled his

tumbler with lemonade and offered Tigg another glassful. "The nursemaid was out in the garden one afternoon two years ago with the son and heir to Lord and Lady Dunsmuir's fortune—the family owns practically the western half of the Canadas, you know, including vast diamond mines, and what they don't own they have interests in—and she fell asleep in the sun. When she woke up, the boy was gone, and despite advertisements, an enormous reward, and the hiring of several Pinkerton men, no one ever discovered what happened."

"Seems clear 'e wandered off. Somebody always 'as to keep an eye on our Willie, not t'mention the Mopsies. Curiosity on legs, every one of 'em."

"He couldn't have wandered off, though," Claire said. "I recall a description of the house that said the garden wall was ten feet high and both gates were locked."

"Eight feet, but yes. My mother says her ladyship was entertaining one of the royal princesses to tea, so the whole household was in an uproar. That's why they'd gone out in the garden. The nursemaid had been hoping the boy would nap in his pram."

"Those poor parents," Claire said on a sigh. "They haven't gone into society since. Lady Dunsmuir, apparently, would walk the roads at night—*asleep*. They have to lock her into her rooms."

Andrew nodded. "My mother eventually gave her notice and retired. She said the sadness was too much to bear."

"Claire?"

A crowd of gentlemen and ladies had come in, chattering like birds, and Claire looked away from Andrew to see Peony Churchill making her way between the tables.

"Claire, it is you! My goodness, where have you been? You're quite the talk of the town." Peony clasped her in a hug, then stood at arms' length and looked her up and down. "You don't look as if you'd been kidnapped, at any rate."

"Certainly not. Peony Churchill, may I present my employer, Mr. Andrew Malvern, and his assistant, Mr. Tigg."

Peony shook hands with both as if it were a matter of course, and Tigg's shoulders went back, as though he were shifting the newfound burden of civility to make it comfortable.

"Will you join us?" Andrew said.

"Oh, no, I won't impose. Besides, that lot will never forgive me—I convinced them to come here when they wanted to go to some awful dive by the river 'just for the adventure.'" Peony rolled her expressive black eyes.

"Your mother is well?" Claire asked eagerly. Isabel Churchill—explorer, noted hostess, and political thorn in the side of many an M.P.—was one of her idols.

"Very well. You remember the Esquimaux delegation?"

"I do. There were so many in the house that the children were sleeping under the dining room table."

"Yes, well, mama was unsuccessful in her pleas on their behalf, so she is preparing an expedition to the north of the Canadas to stir up as much trouble as she can in the diamond mines."

Claire clasped her hands in sheer admiration. "She'll be organizing labor unions among the Esquimaux next."

"I'm sure that's part of her plan—conditions in the mines are dreadful. I'm to go with her, you know. Now that I've graduated, there's no earthly reason to hang about in London."

"Aren't you going to have a Season?" With a jolt, Claire remembered that she was to have been presented to Her Majesty to begin her own Season ... when? Oh, dear. What week was this?

"Me? Dance with a lot of boys who have more air in their heads than *Persephone* herself? Present company excepted, of course," she added hastily as Andrew choked on a mouthful of lemonade.

"Oo's Per Seffonie?" Tigg whispered to Claire.

"The transcontinental airship we were talking about earlier," she whispered back. "The one that goes from here to Paris to New York and Buenos Aires."

"I haven't the least interest in a Season," Peony went on. "But I am taking flying lessons. There will be no one to tell me I can't be an aviatrix in the Canadas."

"I don't imagine there is anyone who can tell you that here, either," Andrew said, smiling at her with such admiration that Claire practically interrupted him to say, "Before you go, Peony, do explain something you said earlier. Why should I be the talk of the town?"

Peony's eyebrows arched in disbelief. "Good heavens, Claire, surely you didn't think you could snub Her Majesty and get away with it?"

Oh, dear. Oh, dear, dear, dear.

"And don't think she didn't notice the resounding silence after your name was called at the Drawing Room last Tuesday. You could hear Julia and Catherine giggling down at the other end of the room, quite clearly."

"Was—was she angry?" And here she'd been worried about her mother's wrath. She'd never thought for a moment she'd provoke the ire of the Queen of the British Empire as well.

"Well, your absence was partly explained by the fact that you are still in mourning. All the same, you won't be getting an invitation to tea anytime soon."

Claire sighed. "It's a lucky thing my social aspirations don't reach those heights, then." Unlike those of her mother, who had taken tea with the queen on more than one occasion.

Claire became aware that both Andrew and Tigg were staring at her as if they'd never seen her before. Peony kissed her and turned in a swirl of bottle-green velvet to join her party, leaving Claire looking from one to the other.

"What is it? Do I have gravy on my chin?"

Tigg found his voice. "Tea? Tea wiv the queen, Lady?"

"I believe the opposite is true. I will not, in fact, be taking tea with the queen, since I appear to have missed my presentation at court."

"Court?" Andrew sounded like an echo. "You were to be presented?"

"Yes. But I was not." *I was too busy burning down my rivals' houses and keeping body and soul together to remember to present myself at Buckingham Palace.*

"But you could have been."

"Yes, of course, had I not been in mourning. Mr. Malvern, please. I am sure Lord James has apprised you of my history and my family. I do regret concealing them from you at first."

Andrew appeared to be struggling to speak, and Tigg just gawked at her. "Yes, he did," he finally said. "And the newspapers augmented the facts with reams of supposition."

The Arabian Bubble. Her father's investment in the ridiculous combustion engine, and its subsequent failure. The Belgrave Riots.

Claire realized she needn't have worried about missing her Season.

She had not been the most eligible catch in London to begin with. Now she might be lucky to get a baron's son, or perhaps a widowed knight with a tumbledown estate and seven cranky children.

How fortunate that marriage had never figured heavily into her plans.

4

When they returned to the laboratory, pleasantly full and with wind-reddened cheeks, Tigg and Andrew stayed below while Claire went upstairs to tackle the next section of the Augean stables.

She and Andrew had agreed that she would work mainly in the mornings, leaving her afternoons free to return to the cottage and keep up the children's lessons. But Tigg seemed to be so absorbed in his work that she didn't have the heart to remove him. She could hear them talking—instructions to "give us another shovel, lad" and "keep an eye on this flame, would you?" sprinkled with explanations of why certain compounds would behave the way they did given certain stimuli. If only that benighted professor at St. Cecilia's had given her the courtesy of explanations instead of merely orders! She might already have earned a University entrance and not needed to take the exams. Instead, she had netted outstanding marks in languages and mathematics, and barely scraped through in Chemistry of the Kitchen, not to mention Social Arts, which had dragged her average down past the point of no return.

Claire tried to keep a cheerful attitude. At least this way she still had a chance to write the entrance examinations in the fall. She was not, after all, in Cornwall.

A loud clank and a shout brought her head up in alarm, and in the next moment she was flying down the stairs. "Mr. Malvern? Tigg? What happened?"

"Nothing," came from under a glass tube as big as a man.

Tigg struggled to lift one end of it long enough to free Andrew from its weight, so she grabbed the other end. Between the two of them, they raised it so that Andrew could roll out from under it. "Good heavens, Mr. Malvern. Are you all right?"

He looked winded, but at the same time, he helped them lower it to the floor. "Gently. It would take a month to make a new one—time we can't afford."

Once they had it safely on the ground, Claire straightened. "How did it come to fall on you?"

"'E were carrying it over to the chamber, and lost 'old of it. Rather than let 'er smash, 'e cushioned it with 'imself." Tigg sounded almost as if he admired this astonishing behavior.

Indeed, the thing must have weighed a hundred pounds.

HER OWN DEVICES

Andrew brushed off his trousers and tugged on his waistcoat before retying his leather apron. "Come, Tigg. I see the error of my ways now. Both of us will carry the tube into the chamber and divide the load. If this tube weighs ninety-two pounds, what will each of our burdens be?"

Tigg thought, even as he hefted one end of the glass onto his shoulder. "This'd be forty-six, sir."

"Excellent. Let us proceed."

Claire followed them into the glassed-in chamber, where instead of hoses waiting to be attached to the tube by metal collars, a series of cables ran into them instead. "What is it for?"

"I have abandoned my efforts to affect the coal's carbon density by external application of chemical gases." Andrew puffed a little and they lowered the tube into its nest of cabling. "My calculations are flawed; there is no way around it. So on further study, I decided to experiment with electrick current."

"But you were using electricks before, were you not?" She had seen the switches; what else could they be? "Are you applying Mr. Tesla's theories?"

"I am. We shall see how prolonged exposure to high levels of current will affect the coal. The best outcome would that it would ossify it, making it last longer and saving the railroad industry millions, especially for long runs."

"Such as wot they 'ave in the Americas," Tigg supplied helpfully, clearly pleased that he could add to her education for once.

Claire nodded, but did not see the glass, or even the

young men in front of her. Instead, she saw a flash of light arcing across a deserted square—saw a man fall, his chest reduced to a smoking ruin. A smoking, hardened ruin. Her mind reeled in the moment that still haunted her. The moment she had, however unintentionally, ended a man's life.

"Claire?"

"Lady?" Tigg touched her arm. "You all right, then?"

She blinked, and instead of the past, the present righted itself all around her. "Yes, thank you, Tigg. I—it was a moment's thought, that's all."

She left them to their labors and returned to hers, but she could no longer concentrate. Something was bothering her about the memory—something more than simply the horror of it. When the afternoon began to wane, she collected her duster and hat and made her way downstairs, brows slightly furrowed.

It would come to her. These mental niggles always did, and found her ready with her engineering notebook and trusty pencil.

They had completed the new assembly, and as she gained the bottom step, Andrew called, "All switches forward?"

"Yes, sir," came Tigg's answer from somewhere away at the back, where it was dark.

"Then let's see how she works." Inside the glass tube, a load of coal waited. Andrew stepped to a control panel at one end of the chamber and threw a lever up. The entire assembly began to hum, and then glow. The glass tube, she saw now, was not completely clear. Within it, channels for current had been embedded, and they glowed an eerie green in the dimness.

"Almost got 'er," Tigg murmured, materializing at her elbow, and Claire had to restrain her instinct to jump.

With a flash, the tube went from green to the familiar yellow of electrick street lamps and the running lights of steambuses. Now the coal itself glowed yellow, as if it were burning within its glass coffin.

Was this the extent of the experiment? Simply to warm it up without causing it to burn? Surely there must be more to all this effort than that.

Andrew threw the switch down. "That stops the electricks, see," Tigg said in a low voice. "It needs to cool, and Mr. Malvern said we'd examine the load in the morning."

Examine the load. Claire restrained the urge to comment on his excellent diction, and said merely, "I see. Are your duties concluded for the day, then?"

"Yes'm. Shall I fire up the boiler?"

"Please." When he opened the door, the daylight made her blink.

"Are you away?" Andrew loped over. "I didn't get a chance to thank you for your work. Both of you." He leaned out to watch Tigg, in the driver's seat, begin the ignition sequence. "He is a very useful young man. I believe our association is going to be productive."

"I hope so. Good night, Mr. Malvern."

"Good night, Lady Claire. Er, do you mind me asking why he abbreviates your title? Tigg, I mean. And I noticed the young ladies do, as well."

She thought fast. "Young Willie cannot manage all the syllables, so he calls me Lady. The others have just

... picked it up, I suppose." Not for worlds would she tell him what it really meant. "They should be thankful that with my brother's elevation to the title, it is no longer proper to call me Miss Trevelyan. Poor Willie. He would never manage."

With a smile and a touch to his goggles that she supposed was meant as some kind of salute, he stepped back and held the door for her. She adjusted her own goggles and arranged her scarf over her hat, tying it securely under her chin and looping the gauzy ends over her shoulders. "Until tomorrow, then."

"I shall look forward to it."

As they navigated the streets home, she reminded herself rather forcefully that he had meant their help with his endeavors.

He did not mean for her to think ... anything more.

At the cottage, Claire ate the sausages and greens that Granny Protheroe had prepared for dinner, deep in thought. She waved the poker players off for another night of civilized marauding in which they would dazzle the gentlemen at the gaming parlors with their prowess at all the new versions of Cowboy Poker. None of their fellow players ever seemed to tumble to the fact that these very boys had invented the hands they were playing. Snouts had told her, laughing, of one indignant lordling who had informed them he studied the hands religiously on the back page of the *Evening Standard*, and since they couldn't have done the same, they must perforce be cheating.

They did not cheat—at least, not that Claire knew of. They were perfectly capable of winning without demeaning themselves by such behavior. It was, in fact, a point of pride with Snouts McTavish.

Fifty percent of the winnings went to her for household expenses and investment, and the player kept the remainder to stake his next game or to spend as he wished. As well, when they had first taken up residence here, they had found a chest full of cash—the proceeds of Lightning Luke's bullying and murdering. In the absence of knowledge of its original owners, Claire had invested half of it, and distributed the rest among everyone remaining in the house, with a substantial donation to the poor-box at the church down the road.

The money had again mounted in the chest upstairs to the point that it now represented a real temptation to someone to inform on them. The Cudgel's waylaying of four of the lads was proof of it. So, that evening, Claire went upstairs and got out paper and ink.

Arundel & Hollis, Solicitors
London SW1

Dear Mr. Arundel,

Thank you for your recent assistance and that of your associates at the stock exchange to purchase shares of the Midlands Railroad and the London Electrick Company for me and for my friends.

I am afraid I must now request your assistance

in a matter of real estate. I should like you to discover the owner of the property containing an abandoned toll booth and a cottage with a walled garden immediately west of the Regent Bridge in Vauxhall Gardens. I am interested in purchasing this property as soon as possible.

Have you had any buyers for the property in Wilton Crescent? Though the house was damaged, the location is very fine. I cannot imagine why it is not selling. I have no doubt you have heard from my mother on the subject, so I will not beleaguer you with it. I was merely curious.

I trust you are well. Again, thank you for all your help.

Sincerely,
Claire Trevelyan

She sealed the letter, popped it in a delivery tube, and turned the codex on the front so that the letters and numbers reflected the solicitor's office address.

Then she reached for another sheet of paper.

Lady Flora St. Ives
Gwynn Place
St. Just in Roseland
Cornwall

Dear Mama,

First, let me assure you that I am well and that

there is no need whatsoever to put advertisements in the papers implying I am missing. I am not missing. Indeed, I am dreadfully embarrassed that you would do such a thing. I am gainfully employed at the laboratory of Mr. Andrew Malvern, Orpington Close, London, who is the partner of Lord James Selwyn. You have received the latter at home in Wilton Crescent, so you may be assured that I am well looked after and by no means unprotected. I have a comfortable home and industrious companionship. You need not worry about me at all.

Mama, I understand that you wish me with you to provide moral support. But I must tell you that there are those here in London who need me just as much, if not more, and whose minds and hearts would be at risk were I to leave them and come to you. I have a position of responsibility and I am well and as happy as can be expected without you and little Nicholas.

Please give my brother a hug and a big kiss for me, and convey my best regards to Polgarth the poultryman. He will be pleased to know his lessons given so many years ago are bearing fruit, as I am shortly to become the owner of half a dozen hens.

I send my love and affection always.

Your daughter,
Claire

There was much more she could have said on the subject of the advertisements, but she restrained herself and rolled the letter up, tucking it in a tube and addressing it. Then she went downstairs, opened the hatch, and with a pneumatic slurp, the Royal Mail system sucked both tubes away into its gullet. In the case of the one to Gwynn Place, it would take a few days to be sorted through the manual switches down to Cornwall, so she had as much as a week to look forward to before she received a reply.

She hoped Mr. Arundel would be much quicker.

That task complete, she fetched the lightning rifle from its concealment beneath the seat of the landau, and sat in the wicker chair outside the back door of the cottage. She laid it across her lap and gazed at it thoughtfully.

A Mopsie popped out the back door like a jack-in-the-box. "Wotcher doin', Lady?"

Since Lizzie never spoke to her voluntarily, this must be Maggie. "I am thinking."

"Wot of?"

"Lightning and electricks and other puzzling things."

"Oh." Maggie lost interest. "Where's our Rosie?"

Claire looked up into the rafters of the rickety porch. Rosie sat perched upon a blackened beam, blending neatly into the shadows now that twilight was upon them. Maggie followed her gaze. "Ah. Gone to bed already. I'd like to know 'ow she gets up there, I would."

"It's the safest place she knows, and I agree with her. She could be snatched if she roosted on the wall, and an otter could come up out of the water and take her if she slept on the ground. All in all, she has used her powers of deduction and found the most suitable spot, as any lady of resources would do."

"I ent never seen 'er fly."

"Chickens will surprise you. How are you coming with your plans for a traveling coop? Did you find supplies today?"

Maggie nodded. "Them folks at the metalworks sure waste a lot. We found pistons and a set of legs. Bit banged up, but useful. T'boys met us by our old squat on t'river and we loaded up the boat."

"Did you find any hens?"

"No, but we didn't get near any of the markets. Tomorrow, Snouts says." A call from the upper floor made her withdraw. "G'night, Lady."

"Good night, Maggie. Sweet dreams."

With only Rosie for company, Claire sat in the gathering dark and let her thoughts drift. This aggravating niggle in her mind had something to do with the lightning. Electricks were yellow for the most part. Or green, sometimes, if there wasn't much current. Andrew was running full current through his glass tube, so its yellow color was perfectly healthy and to be expected.

Then why ...?

Why was the firing charge from the lightning rifle white edged with blue?

What was the difference?

Electricks had never harmed anyone. They were strictly for domestic and industrial use. The glass tube had got hot, but the current itself was not dangerous.

Then why had one blast from this rifle been able to kill a man? Was it hundreds of times stronger than ordinary electricks? Or was it a different kind altogether—something only the builder of this weapon knew?

She needed to lay the rifle before Andrew Malvern and ask these questions. She needed to know what the difference in color and power signified—and more important, how it was created. The cell in the rifle did not seem any different than those that powered household items like the mother's helper, which cleaned the floors using kinetick energy.

What made this so different? So lethal?

Andrew would—

No. She could not bring this to Andrew. While he might not know who Lightning Luke was or how he'd come by his moniker, he would certainly know that gently reared ladies of Blood families did not go about with deadly weapons in their soft, gloved hands.

Claire set her teeth.

Blast it all. She needed to know.

Just how much was she going to allow convention to dictate her behavior when it clearly obstructed the path to knowledge?

HER OWN DEVICES

5

Tigg managed to control his impatience long enough for her to climb out of the landau and join him at the door, but once inside, he bounded across the warehouse floor. Andrew had already arrived and was just removing the collar from the glass tube.

"Did it work, sir?" he asked as Claire removed her duster.

"You mustn't expect anything to work the first time, Tigg," Andrew said as Claire joined them. "Give me a hand with this, will you?"

Together they set the tube on the floor and Andrew reached in for a handful of coal.

"Looks ezackly the same as when we put it in, sir."

Andrew looked crestfallen. "You're quite correct."

With a hammer, he tapped the coal and it broke into several pieces. "There is no difference. It is neither harder nor more brittle. It just ... is." He sighed. "Well, such is the nature of science. I must turn my mind to a different approach, that's all."

"What if the nature of the electricks is the trouble?" Claire asked from behind them.

Andrew and Tigg turned, as if surprised to see her there. "The nature of them?" Andrew repeated.

"Is there not a different kind of electrick you might apply? One that is ... stronger, perhaps?"

"I'm afraid the City of London can't supply anything stronger," Andrew said. "In fact, along with the steam engine that powers it, I have a number of converters in the system of this chamber that would not be, er, approved by our good Commissioner of Works, because they increase the current to a point that is too dangerous for ordinary use. Hence the glass chamber. I do not want my laboratory burning down."

"Mr. Malvern ..." She stopped. She must tread carefully. "What might it mean if an electrick current were not yellow or green, but blue-white?"

Tigg looked at her strangely, but to his credit, said not a word.

"Where have you seen such a thing?" Andrew frowned at her in a most disconcerting way. "Even Mr. Tesla's cells do not produce blue-white current. They are always yellow."

"But what would it mean?"

"Why, it would mean a stronger concentration of power than any I've ever seen."

Strong enough to kill a man on contact.

"In fact, I read a paper once about a device that could generate such a current, but the engineering was a cross between genius and fantasy. Even if such a device existed any longer, it would be so dangerous that no one could work with it for fear of being killed."

"It did exist at one time?"

"It must have. One must submit one's inventions to the Royal Society of Engineers and have them vetted in order to have one's papers published."

"Do you know who might have written it?" A name would give her a place to start in mining his office for that paper.

Andrew laughed. "I do, but it won't do any of us any good. You heard me say it was a combination of fantasy and genius?"

"The genius part might be interesting to us."

"There is a fine line between genius and madness in some people, I'm afraid. The author of this particular paper is no longer with us."

Claire's shoulders wilted in disappointment. "He's dead, then?"

"She. And no, she's not dead. She is in Bedlam."

"A scientist in Bedlam, sir? Insane?" Even Tigg sounded shocked.

"I'm afraid so. She was committed years ago, when she attacked Sir George Longmont, the Chief Engineer, at a meeting of the Royal Society. I was not present— being still a schoolboy then—but the old-timers told me it was a horrific scene. She had been one of the very first women admitted to the Society, you see. When she was committed, it set the Wits back twenty years."

Claire suppressed a shudder. If the lady had been committed to the Bethlehem Royal Hospital years ago, it meant she was housed in the Incurable ward. Most people were cured and released in a year or less. Only the truly insane were locked away for their own good and that of society.

Andrew gazed at the coal in his hand. "Such a waste of an amazing mind. The electricks were all destroyed, for safety. Or almost all. A few went missing but they've never turned up. I supposed we'd know it if they did—it would be difficult to miss explosions or buildings suddenly burning down."

Goosebumps prickled on Claire's shoulders. "What would happen if one did turn up?"

Andrew laughed. "The likelihood of anyone knowing what to do with such a thing would be low."

"I knew a man once," Tigg said. "'E's dead now, o' course, but they say 'e got into college afore 'e frew it all away an' turned to a life of crime. Handy wiv electricks, 'e was." Tigg studiously avoided looking at Claire.

"I wouldn't like to see one of these devices in the hands of a criminal," Andrew said slowly. "Fortunately, they were small. Dr. Craig—that was the scientist's name, Rosemary Craig—could carry one in her reticule and still have room for stamps and a pocketbook."

"But if there was a big 'un?" Tigg asked. "What then?"

Andrew gazed at his chamber. "From what I remember, even a small cell could probably power this chamber."

"Could you build one?" Claire asked. "If you could find that paper?"

He shook his head. "Not if the order was given to destroy them. Once the Society makes that decision, it's final. Every copy of the paper in their archives would have been destroyed. Now that I recall, it was that order that triggered the attack on the Chief Engineer. Dr. Craig simply snapped."

Claire wondered if she might not do the same in that unfortunate lady's position. Imagine devoting your life to a magnificent device, creating it, demonstrating it—and then being told that it was dangerous and every example of it would be destroyed. Flying at the Chief Engineer, it seemed to her, would be a fairly reasonable response.

But perhaps every example had not been destroyed.

The lightning rifle. Could it really be that it contained one of Rosemary Craig's lost devices? And if it did, how could Claire find a way to use it to help Andrew in his endeavors?

The trouble was, she did not know enough about electricks. She could show the rifle to him, but then she would run into the troublesome problem of telling him where she'd got it. And that was impossible.

No. She needed to learn more about Rosemary Craig and what she had created. But how? Where?

Claire went upstairs and began work on the piles of treatises, formulae, and measurements to one side of the desk. As she sorted, she began to see patterns—in the paperwork, in names, and in the nature of Andrew's experiments. And in the back of her mind, a resolution formed.

Dr. Craig must have had a family. And if it were a respectable family, no one would know more about them than their staff. And no one knew more people among the servants in the great houses than Mrs. Morven, the Trevelyans' former cook at Wilton Crescent.

She was now employed by Lord James Selwyn at Hanover Square, but Claire would not allow that to dissuade her. Lord James was away, and there was nothing to prevent her from visiting a well-loved former employee, now, was there?

Mrs. Morven opened the door so fast that Claire was sure she'd been waiting behind it for her to knock. "My dear Lady Claire!" She had never been given to displays of affection, but she swept Claire into a hug against her vast chest and kissed her soundly on both cheeks.

Claire kissed her back, adjusted her hat, and stepped inside Lord James's home. It smelled of carnations and furniture polish. "It's very good to see you, Mrs. Morven. Lord James is treating you well?"

As she spoke, she took in every detail. Parquet floor in the hall. Ah, there were the carnations, in the front parlor, which was tastefully decorated in Wedgewood blue and Nile green. Not a speck of dust lay anywhere, from walls painted cream to the furniture and woodwork. Whoever was keeping house for him was a paragon. Claire thought of her own rough-and-tumble lot in the cottage, its table stained from chemical experiments, its floors coated with drying mud no matter how often they swept.

Never mind. It was full of life, not this dignified silence that spoke of the absence of both master and friends.

"Yes, my lady, he treats the staff very well. Always courteous, always a gentleman. It's very quiet, though, I must say. Not as much life as on Wilton Crescent. I wonder how the little viscount, your brother, is getting on?"

"He is well," Claire said, hoping it was the truth. "My mother owes me a letter, so I'll have news of him shortly, I'm sure."

"And her ladyship?"

"Also well." *You didn't happen to see an advertisement with my face on it, did you?* Never mind. It would be better not to ask.

"Come into my parlor." Mrs. Morven waved her into a cozy little room down the stairs, opposite her office, where tea was already set out. "When I got your tube this morning, I was glad I'd done a little baking. I hope you still like orange chiffon cakes."

Claire nearly swooned. Beside the cook's lemon soufflé, the little orange cakes iced in melted chocolate were her favorite. "You must have the second sight. I believe I dreamed about these last night."

Pleased, Mrs. Morven poured tea for them both and handed her a cup. "Now, miss—er, I mean, Lady Claire—I must say it's glad I am to be seeing you safe and well. After the riots I had my doubts about your safety. That one little note you sent wasn't very comforting."

"I am very well. In fact, I had lunch yesterday in Piccadilly and met Peony Churchill at the restaurant. She remarked upon the same thing."

"Gorse was inquiring after you, too. I'm glad I can tell him I've seen you with my own eyes, and you're hale and hearty."

"Do give him my best regards, and let him know I have a student of mechanics now myself who will be every bit his equal when he grows up. Is Gorse ... happy at Wellesley House?" Claire hoped so. But in her mind, even the joys of a four-piston landau in the mews would not make up for having to work for Julia Wellesley's family. *Insufferable Blood arrogance* did not do them justice.

"He seems so. But then, his heart being away down there in Cornwall, I don't suppose he cares much where the rest of him is."

Poor Gorse. "I still don't understand why he didn't toss the second footman off the Flying Dutchman and go with Silvie, if he's in love with her."

Mrs. Morven smiled at her fondly. "Ah, the young. You think that love is worth throwing over a good situation and the prospects of a stable life. Gorse is old enough to know he must be able to provide a home for Silvie. Working at Wellesley House will let him do that. Working in the carriage house at Gwynn Place, your lady mother's circumstances being what they are, would not."

"I know." Claire sighed. "You're quite right. I shall

look forward to a wedding in any case." If her mother would ever let Silvie go. A French lady's maid who could detect every whiff of fashion that came out of Paris and duplicate it with materials on hand was not easy to come by.

"So, miss, now that I know you're well and you know that we're well, perhaps you can tell me what that mysterious line in your note was all about? You wanted to 'mine my memories,' or some such."

"I did." Claire placed her teacup in its saucer, noting that it was none other than the third best set from Wilton Crescent. At least some of their things had survived the riots. "I would like to know if you know anything of the Craig family—specifically, the family of a scientist called Rosemary Craig, who I am given to understand is one of the unfortunates in Bedlam."

Mrs. Morven took a long sip of tea and rocked herself gently in her chair. "A sad story, that."

"I have heard some of it. Do you know the family?"

"I did once. My cousin was engaged to their butler, back when they could afford him."

"And now?" Claire prompted, hoping that was not the end of it.

"Well, they did wind up getting married, but not until he took another situation. After Miss Craig was committed, the family withdrew from society. Shame, too. Apparently there was a sister about to make her come-out, and when that didn't happen, the story is she went a little mad herself."

"I can't imagine driving oneself mad over missing a debut."

"Begging your pardon, miss, but you aren't like most young ladies in town. You know as well as me that some prepare their entire lives for their Season."

That was true enough. If Julia Wellesley had put half as much energy into improving her mind as she did in improving her appearance, she might have gained a man's respect instead of settling for his admiration. "Perhaps there was more to it. Is the family still in town?"

"Oh, aye. Last I heard from my cousin, they had taken a house in Chelsea. They're a little more bohemian down there."

Madness in the family being a social advantage to that lot, Claire heard as clearly as if she'd said it. Mrs. Morven would die sooner than take employment anywhere outside the black iron fences of Belgravia or Kensington.

A rattle of hooves and the sound of wheels coming to a stop on the pavement outside caused them both to lift their heads. "Bless me," Mrs. Morven said. "I hope that's not his lordship. We weren't expecting him back until Thursday. The butler has the day off."

A rush of feet in the hall above told Claire the parlor maid had gone to answer the door. "If it is his lordship I won't stay. I'll just slip out and—"

"Oh, no, miss. He'd be terrible offended if you slipped away without a proper greeting. Talks of you all the time, he does."

I'll bet. "Truly, no, I'm sure he'll be tired and wishing to—"

A deep, cultivated voice in the hall above mingled

with the parlor maid's treble tones. And before Claire could gather up her hat and reticule and flee, the girl had appeared in the doorway. "Excuse me, Lady Claire. His lordship says what a pleasure and can he see you in the library. Mrs. Morven, ma'am, he asks for some refreshment."

"A gentleman's refreshment, or the kind fit for my young lady, here?"

The girl hesitated, her gaze darting from Claire to the older woman. "He didn't say, ma'am."

"I shall send both, then. Millie, show Lady Claire to the library. By the time you come back, I'll have a tray ready."

Oh, dear. This was intolerable. Claire mounted the stairs much the way she was sure Mary, Queen of Scots, must have climbed the steps to the block at Fotheringhay. She should have run while she had the chance. She shouldn't have come at all. Why couldn't she merely have sent a note and asked any further questions by correspondence? What had she been thinking?

"Lady Claire Trevelyan, your lordship," the parlor maid squeaked, like a violin played by an inexperienced hand, and Claire walked in to face the one man she despised above every other person on earth.

6

He turned from his contemplation of the vase of paper flowers that filled the cold hearth in the summer. It had been not quite two weeks since he had attempted to blackmail her, and the force of those emotions under Claire's breastbone had not yet had time to diminish.

She had no idea of his thoughts. He stood, still in his traveling clothes, and regarded her as though she were there to collect funds for charity. Well, whatever his behavior, her family dated back to the fourteenth century, and she would not disgrace her breeding by alluding to his defects of character.

Perhaps his was only a life peerage. One must make allowances.

"Lord James," she said politely, when it was clear

that though he had summoned her, he did not seem inclined to speak. "I trust you had a good journey?"

"Very good," he said, a little absently.

"I am happy to hear it. You were meeting with railroad people, I understand."

"Yes." His gaze sharpened. "And you have been talking with Andrew."

"He is my employer," she said steadily. "We talk quite frequently, given that I am in his office four hours a day at least."

A knock sounded and Millie came in with a tray. She set out the teapot and cups—Limoges, no third best services here—yet more orange chiffon cake, and a decanter of spirits.

When the door closed behind her, he said, "Would you like some tea?"

"No, thank you. I have been visiting Mrs. Morven and we—"

"Then I hope you won't object if I have a drink."

Definitely a life peerage.

"I'm sure you're tired after your long absence. I won't trouble you." She turned for the door, when the sound of a glass being set hard on the table startled her into turning back. Reflex had her reaching over her shoulder for the lightning rifle, and when she realized what she was doing, she turned it into a self-conscious maneuver with her hatpin.

"Lady Claire." He splashed whiskey into the abused glass, but did not pick it up. "I find that in spite of my express wishes, you have accepted employment with my partner. He sent a tube two days ago to tell me you had begun work. I want to know why."

Because the Lady of Devices does not bow to black-mail.

"When we last spoke I told you I would do so. I must keep a roof over my head, sir. As you know perfectly well."

"You have an adequate roof at Carrick House."

"The house is for sale, and after the riots it is uninhabitable. Roofs notwithstanding, I fail to see why my working for your partner should be so objectionable."

"You know why."

The temptation to swing the decanter at his head surged through her, and she mastered it. "I do not. Please enlighten me."

His fingers closed around the glass so tightly the liquid vibrated. "It is inconceivable to me that a woman I had hoped to court should be working for me. There. Is that plain enough for you?"

He had said something very like that during the disastrous interview. "It is inconceivable to me that you should harbor such a hope, sir. I knew nothing of it. And even if I had, it would not have stopped me. I want to work for your partner. I need to learn from him."

"And charm him into giving up his secrets?"

She glanced at the decanter. Heavy crystal. A couple of pounds at least.

"I shall not need to use charm, even if I were silly enough to stoop to it. I am filing thousands of papers, and I'm perfectly capable of reading what interests me. Is there something you wish me not to see?"

"Andrew is doing valuable work. Any one of the treatises he has written could be sold."

"And you believe me capable of that?"

He took a breath, as if to answer, and let it out again. "I have no idea what you're capable of."

We are in complete agreement there.

"I must have your word, Lady Claire, that nothing you learn in our laboratory will leave it. Nothing, do you understand?"

She looked him dead in the eye. Snouts McTavish would have run to the far side of the garden had he seen that look, knowing that a bolt of lightning was about to follow.

"You insult me, sir, by insisting on such a promise. Of course I would not speak of what I learn in the laboratory. Nor would Tigg, or the—" She almost said *Mopsies*, but stopped herself in time. "—or any of the children."

"Those children are not to come on my property!"

"Mr. Malvern has already given his permission."

"Then I rescind it."

"Why?"

He stared at her. "Why? Because children have no place there, that's why. They could be hurt, or destroy something, or—"

"Tigg is already acting as Mr. Malvern's assistant, and very capably, too. Are you telling me you plan to deprive him of a way to better himself? Can you really be that unkind?"

Now he was entirely speechless. She took advantage of the welcome silence.

"If I had ever harbored any tender feelings toward you, my lord, this interview would have put paid to them. A man of your stature should be able to extend charity to those less fortunate, especially if it comes at no cost to himself. If Andrew is willing to teach him, how can you tell him he may not learn?"

"You ... are a Wit," he snapped.

She smiled. "How observant of you, sir. But my question stands."

She had shamed him. His face flushed, and it was fortunate the glass was made of stern stuff, or it would have shattered in his grip long ago.

"Your father would be ashamed of you."

"My father is dead, and I have good reason to be ashamed of him."

"You are the most unladylike young woman I have ever had the misfortune to meet."

"You have not answered me, my lord."

"You will not hold me hostage with your infernal questions."

"But you are free to blackmail me with impunity?"

She had brought out the bull in him. He practically pawed the Turkish carpet. He towered over her by at least a foot, and could probably snap her in two if he laid hands on her, and yet she would not back down. A year ago she would have burst into tears at the very sight of him, and run to her room.

The Lady of Devices did not run from anyone.

He controlled his temper by gritting his teeth and breathing deeply. "I shall write to your mother."

She could stand up to Lightning Luke Jackson. She

could take on The Cudgel without fear. But this ... this! This was beyond anything.

"Why should you do that?" she said between stiff lips.

"To rescind the letter I sent her three weeks ago."

Three weeks ago? Before he had tried to force her to turn down Andrew's offer of employment? "What letter?"

"The one in which I told her my intentions toward you were honorable, and asked her permission to court you. I certainly have no desire to do so now, and you have made it abundantly clear that the feeling is mutual."

Now it was her turn to stare at him, jaw unhinged. She must look like she belonged in Bedlam herself. "You—you did *what*?"

"You didn't believe me, did you, when I interrupted your interview with Andrew? I can assure you, when I wrote that letter I was in earnest. Despite the fact that you no longer have a dowry, and you are certainly not the catch you were in June, I was still prepared to make an honorable offer. Lord knows you could use a firm hand on the reins."

She overlooked these insulting remarks while she calculated time versus the speed of the mail system. Her mother had sent a letter saying she would be dragged bodily down to Cornwall if she didn't come voluntarily. Lord James's letter had obviously crossed with it. No wonder she had not heard again. Lady St. Ives was probably shouting hallelujah and planning the wedding.

Lord James wanted to court her. To marry her. Lord

James Selwyn.

It beggared understanding.

"But—but why?" If he had been Fermat's theorem made flesh, she couldn't have been any more stumped.

"Why should I want to court you and contemplate a life in your company? I agree, it's quite astonishing."

"All the more reason I should want to know."

He put the glass down carefully on the mantel, and studied the paper flowers as if they had been freshly delivered from the Antipodes. "Because you almost won at Cowboy Poker on your first try. Because no matter how abominably those meringues treat you, you are unfailingly polite. Because, Lady Claire, you have a spine."

"You did not seem to appreciate my spine a few minutes ago."

"I have a temper. Sometimes it gets the better of me."

A gentleman of breeding could control his emotions. Claire let it pass. "Meringues?"

"Those girls. Julia and Catherine and that Astor featherhead."

"You are most uncomplimentary, sir." Meringues. Sweet on the outside but having absolutely no substance within. She bit down on the urge to giggle.

"It's a failing of mine," he said on a sigh, then glanced up. "It does not seem to have had much effect on you."

I have killed a man, however unintentionally. Uncomplimentary remarks no longer have the effect they used to.

"Are you a life peer, sir?"

He looked a little surprised. "No. Selwyns have held lands and the title in Derbyshire since 1625. Why?"

She shook her head. "No reason. I must thank you for your good intentions, Lord James, at the very least. Send your letter if you must."

"I think I must. Unless you would like us to—I mean, if you wanted me to—what I mean to say is—"

He broke off, floundering, his face reddening as he realized he had left himself open to the lash of her tongue—and her poor opinion.

Several thoughts flashed through her mind with the force of a lightning storm.

Despite his fearsome denials, he might just want to go through with it after all.

If it were known he was courting her, she would be safe from public opinion.

She could continue her activities at night, and no one would connect the infamous Lady with the intended of Lord James Selwyn.

He did not love her. So when she must inevitably break it off, he would not be hurt.

And it would deal such a poke in the eye to Julia and Catherine and all the rest that they would never recover. She would be the first of her class at school to become engaged. She, the one with no prospects—indeed, who was more familiar with social disgrace than social graces—would be the first to be chosen.

She returned from that far-off, sparkling vista to realize that he was gazing at her, waiting, while the color returned to normal in his face. He must be preparing himself to be soundly refused.

"I must be permitted to continue my work in your laboratory," she heard herself say.

It took him a moment to realize what she meant. "I see that I have no power to stop you, short of hammering a sheet of wood over the door."

"I am responsible for the children."

"Curiosity compels me to ask about them, but I will save it for another time."

"You will not visit me at home."

"That would be most improper."

"I shall be applying to The University of London, to begin classes in the autumn."

"Claire—"

"I am immovable on this point."

"This is the deal breaker?"

"It is, sir."

"It will be a very long engagement, in that case."

"Four years. Three, if I take advanced classes and study during the summers."

He did not drop his gaze. "I find this a very strange turn of events. I had every intention of turning you out of the house."

"That would have been beneath you, sir."

"James. If we are to be engaged, you must call me by my name."

She didn't think she could force her tongue to shape the word. Instead, she tugged on her gloves and held out her hand. "I must be going. Thank you for ... er, tea."

"I won't write to Cornwall, then." He sounded as if

he wanted confirmation that they had just done what he thought they'd done.

"Only to tell my mother the ... happy news. Or no, perhaps I should do that."

"If you would. Well ... goodbye, then. For now."

"Goodbye, Lord James."

It wasn't until she was in the Underground carriage that the consequences of what she'd done hit her.

An old lady sitting across the aisle was kind enough to lend her a handkerchief to wipe up her tears.

7

She must have been mad.

She would write to Lord James when she got home this evening and call the whole thing off. And then she would write to her mother and tell her she had called the whole thing off. And then Lady St. Ives would be on the next train to London. Oh dear, oh dear.

Claire leaned her head back against the window of the coach and closed her eyes in despair, which meant she nearly missed her Underground stop.

Surfacing from the tunnel into the bright light of late afternoon, she waited for her eyes to adjust. If she went back to the cottage now, she would only have to make the trip to Chelsea another day. Granted, at the moment finding out about Dr. Rosemary Craig seemed trivial, compared to what Claire had just done to herself. On the other hand, having a concrete task to perform might serve as a distraction, giving her a little distance until she was able to think clearly.

A brief stop at the local switch of the Royal Mail provided her with the location of the Craig house, which turned out to be a flat on the third floor of a building crammed between two more prosperous ones. So the Craigs did not go about in society? Claire wondered whether they could even squeeze outside.

It wasn't until she stood at the door that she remembered she should have sent up a card first, to make sure the inhabitants were at home to visitors. However, in the absence of anyone to send a card up *with*, she herself would have to do.

At her knock, the door swung wide and she found herself face to face with a woman in her thirties wearing a severe gray suit in the elaborately bustled style of the previous decade.

"Good afternoon," Claire said in her best social tones. "I am Lady Claire Trevelyan, and I do apologize for not informing you of my visit. Do I have the pleasure of addressing Miss Craig?"

The woman wobbled a bit at the knees, as if she were unsure whether or not to curtsey. Claire extended a hand and shook with the other woman to set her at ease. Finally she said, "I am Dorothy Craig. Please, won't you come in?"

The furniture was so glossy with polish that one might almost miss the threadbare condition of the cushions. The floor likewise shone, and the single carpet was a good Persian. Daguerreotype photographs in silver frames were arranged upon a sideboard, and Claire wondered if Dr. Rosemary Craig's likeness was among them.

"Would you like some tea?" Dorothy asked.

"Thank you, but no. I won't trespass on your kindness. I merely came to inquire about a woman I believe is your sister. Doctor Rosemary Craig."

At the word *sister*, the expression of polite but puzzled interest froze into shock. Claire hastened on, despite the sinking feeling in her stomach that she had made a mistake. "I am very much interested in your sister's work for—for a paper I am working on, and—" The other woman stood. "Miss Craig?"

"I am very sorry to incommode you, Lady Claire, but I find I have a headache coming on. Please allow me to show you out."

How odd. She didn't have any of the symptoms Mama exhibited during one of her headaches—the pale skin, the wincing at noise, the inability to bear light.

"I am very sorry to be the cause of your headache," she said gently. "I will go, but I hope you will answer one question. Did your sister leave behind any papers or information that I might look at for my research?"

"If she did, they were burned years ago," Dorothy said, her voice tight. "Before she was sent away."

"To Bedlam."

"It's common knowledge among the titled, is it—my family's disgrace?" she said bitterly.

"Not at all. I learned of it from someone at the Royal Society of Engineers. I mean—not the disgrace, which I am sure is not true, but of your sister's unfortunate circumstances."

"Which brought on our disgrace. My father was only a barrister, but who will hire a man into a position of trust when madness runs in his family?"

Claire saw that there were closed doors down a miniscule corridor on her right. "Are your parents well?"

"My mother passed away two years ago. I am my father's nurse. As you see—" Her voice trembled, but whether with grief or rage, Claire couldn't tell. "—our family has not recovered."

Claire's own family had not recovered from disgrace, either, but one did not simply sit down and give up. "Do you see your sister?" she asked softly, fully expecting to be pushed out the door.

"Oh, yes. Once a month, faithful as can be. For all the good it does."

"Does she not recognize you?"

"Certainly. And therein lies the trouble. She blames us, you see, for having her committed. In her mad mind, she is perfectly sane and we are the crazy ones." She turned away and picked up one of the pictures. "I don't know why my father keeps this." She handed it to Claire.

A young woman with dark hair piled high and wearing a tightly corseted gown stood to one side of a Greek pillar. One hand rested on the plinth, while the other held what appeared to be a key. The key of knowledge, one assumed. Indeed, her face was fierce, her eyes dark and intense, as if she were daring the photographer to get on with it; she had work to do. This was the face of a woman who would indeed fly at a man for getting in her way.

"Thank you for showing me." She handed it back. "So she is allowed visitors?"

"Family only. Who else would want to see what her brains have made of her? And of the rest of us."

Any empathy Claire might have felt was fast draining away. This woman was not crippled, nor was she lacking in intelligence. She could make her own way if it had not been more rewarding to blame someone else for her misfortunes.

"I appreciate your time." Claire extended her hand again. "Good afternoon."

She walked back to the Embankment as fast as she could, thankful for her escape from that narrow house. So Dr. Rosemary Craig was permitted family visitors, was she? Well, it was clear that Claire was not going to get any information from outside sources. Perhaps the poor lady in Bedlam would enjoy a visit from her long-lost cousin from Shropshire.

Express Mail
For Immediate Delivery

My dear Claire,

    I am this moment in receipt of your tube. We will not discuss the advertisement—I was driven to it by desperation. I wish to speak of happier topics.

HER OWN DEVICES

As you can imagine, since I received Lord James's letter two weeks ago I have been all aflutter. It was everything I could do not to buy a train ticket and come up to town immediately. Now I know why you have been so reluctant to join me here at Gwynn Place.

You sly minx, prating on about charitable works when all the time you have been indulging in a whirlwind flirtation with Lord James! I must credit your taste, if not your experience.

Let me advise you, dear. Accept only invitations from your closest circle. Due to our circumstances you were not able to make your curtsey to Her Majesty, so that means you must begin your Season with decorum. You may attend the theatre in Lord James's company, and small dinners, but resist the temptation to be seen at any balls but those of the kind I might have attended with your dear father. Countess Selkirk, the Duchess of Wellesley, Lady Mount-Batting ... these are the best hostesses and are the only invitations you should accept.

I will place the announcement of your engagement in the Times this week. I will also write to Mr. Arundel to see if there is any possibility of a sum to settle upon you. Lord James has been very generous—I have read between the lines and he is quite prepared to take you in nothing but your petticoat— ah, young love!—but there must be something, somewhere, in the accounts. What are we to have a wedding dress made with, else?

Nicholas sends a kiss, and Polgarth the poultry-

man begs me to advise you that each bird must have eighteen inches of roosting space in the coop. I do not know what this means, but I am dutifully passing it on.

I will let this do. Please write soonest and tell me of your plans. I must have a wedding date to put in the announcement. And do have Lord James bring you down for a visit within the month. I want to get to know him better.

Ever your loving
Mama

Claire rolled up the lavender-scented paper and tossed it in the fire burning merrily in the cottage's hearth. Willie turned big eyes on her and then climbed up the arm of the rickety sofa and into her lap.

"You oughtn't to waste good paper, Lady," Lizzie informed her. "Even Willie knows that."

"It was a letter from my mother, and I did not wish its contents seen."

"We wouldn't've looked. I could 'ave done another drawing of our walking coop on the back. An' it smelled nice, it did."

"Perhaps Granny Protheroe will teach you how to make lavender water, so that you may have your own."

Lizzie subsided, mumbling something that Claire chose not to hear.

Cuddling Willie, who with regular meals was beginning to sprout out of his clothes, she raised her voice and spoke to the chemists at the table, the girls before the hearth, and the poker players, who had not yet left for the evening. "Has anyone ever been to Bedlam?"

The room had been lively with chatter, but now it fell silent. "Bedlam, Lady?" Lewis asked. "As in visited, or as in committed?"

"As in visited, silly gumpus. I wish to visit one of the patients there and I should like to know what it's like beforehand."

Jake and one of the chemists looked at one another. "Me gran said once that they used t'sell tickets so folk could come and gawk at the lunatics."

"Yes, well, they do not do so in this enlightened age," Claire said crisply.

Jake was not finished. "I been, oncet. And I'm not like to go again. It were hellish, it were."

"How so, Jake?" She did not like to ask whom he had been visiting, in case it was a sensitive subject.

"People rambling up and down the galleries, some in proper clothes, some in nightclothes—some in nowt at all. People screamin', beggin' fer help. It were awful."

Claire swallowed. "Tigg and I have learned that the scientist who invented the device that powers the lightning rifle is in Bedlam. I wish to speak with her about it."

Jake shook his head. "You'll do as you like, o' course, Lady, but me, I wouldn't. No device is worth goin' there again."

"I'll go with you," Tigg said quietly, appearing out of the dark hallway, out of range of the lamps and firelight.

"Not wi'out me," Snouts said, his nose throwing a

vulture-like shadow on the wall behind him. "Mopsies? Ready for a mission?"

Sitting on the rug before the hearth, the girls looked at each other, then back at Claire. They shook their heads as one. "Not we, Lady," Maggie said. "I'm afraid o' them lunatics."

Claire nodded with understanding. "Very well. Snouts and Tigg will accompany me. The scientist's name is Doctor Rosemary Craig, therefore, I shall be her cousin, Lady Claire Craig, from Shropshire. Snouts and Tigg shall be my secretary and his assistant. Perhaps you might lay hands on a pair of spectacles, Snouts, to complete the illusion."

"I b'lieve I 'ave some, Lady. Won 'em in a hand of poker not long back. Nice gold rims on 'em."

"Perfect. We shall go tomorrow."

Tigg and Snouts nodded, then faded into the dark. They had first watch tonight. Willie's body had relaxed in her lap, and when she looked down, she saw he had fallen asleep. She carried him upstairs, which meant she didn't see the Mopsies grab the poker and fish what was left of her mother's letter out of the grate.

HER OWN DEVICES

8

The sound of the warehouse door closing below brought Andrew out of his fierce concentration on a recent paper on the augmentation of electricks for industrial use. He had not heard the arrival of the landau, nor was that the swish of skirts on the stairs. In any case, Claire would not come so late at night.

It could only be— "Hello, James."

James Selwyn mounted the last of the stairs into the lamplight and smiled. "Hard at work, I see. I thought you might be." His gaze touched on the desk, the floor, a cabinet. "Something is different up here."

"You're seeing the initial results of Claire's influence." Andrew spread his hands to indicate the top of his desk. "I hardly dare leave a piece of paper out in case I get a lecture in the morning."

"You are her employer," James said dryly. He went to the table by the window and poured himself a finger of Scotch. "You could tell her to dispense with the lecture."

"Ah, but then I would be deprived of the pleasure of it. How did it go at the Midlands Railroad?"

James took a healthy sip before speaking, and grimaced as the liquor went down. "Not so well, I am afraid. They appreciate the possibilities of what we're doing—in fact, they're quite enthusiastic about it. But they are not willing to promise to buy one of our devices without having seen it in action."

He'd told James he was premature, but when had James ever listened when it came to his vision for their partnership? "You can hardly blame them for that. You and I would both do the same."

"Perhaps. But we need a large railroad to back our efforts and give us legitimacy. Rail men are notorious for presenting a united front, competitive as they might be behind it. If we can crack only one, we'll have them all."

"I told you it was too soon. We must have a working prototype before we approach anyone."

James merely shrugged. "How are the experiments coming? Any progress?"

Andrew had to shake his head. "I have given up on permeating the coal with gases and have turned my attention to augmented electricks. Hence a little research." He indicated the paper. "Claire seems to think that—"

"Claire? What does she have to do with anything?"

Andrew raised an eyebrow. James was too well bred

to interrupt ... usually. But Claire had been the clinker in his coal box ever since the day they'd met. "You know she aspires to be an engineer."

"I do, to my very great dismay."

"I have promised to help her get into university in any way I can. And that usually means talking over problems together." James merely snorted and emptied his glass. "Don't you have any confidence in her?"

"My confidence or lack of it is irrelevant. The girl was hired to shuffle paper, not offer uninformed opinions on a great work."

"Her opinions are far from uninformed. She came up with a theory that I feel I must explore, in fact."

"Ridiculous. Next you'll be holding her yarn for her while she knits."

"I don't believe the lady does knit," Andrew said coolly. "And I must say I don't understand your attitude toward her."

"Yes, you do. I've told you before."

"That you had honorable intentions and now cannot bear to see her in a position of dependence on us—on you?"

"That would sum it up, yes. And the fact that I seem completely powerless to stop her."

Andrew was not a man who normally pried into his friend's private life, but this was too much for him. "Why should you want to stop her, James? If she has declined your attentions and yet is a valuable addition to this venture, what has it to do with you any longer?"

James appeared to be struggling with himself. "You're going to find out anyway," he muttered.

"I beg your pardon?"

He raised his head and lifted his empty glass in a toast. "Congratulate me, Andrew," he said in a tone that approximated good cheer. "I am going to embrace the proverbial ball and chain in, oh, four years or so."

Perplexed, Andrew stared at him. "For the love of heaven, James, what on earth are you talking about?"

"Simply this. Much to my astonishment, and without quite knowing how it came about, I have somehow found myself engaged to your laboratory assistant."

Was James so exhausted that a single finger of whiskey had addled his brain? "I don't understand you." Andrew's lips felt frozen, his tongue barely able to form the words.

"Let me rephrase. This afternoon I believe I proposed to Lady Claire Trevelyan, and I am nearly perfectly certain she accepted."

Andrew felt his jaw unhinge—and his mind as well. He simply could not make reality and this new information match in any way that was sane.

"Yes, I feel much the same way," James went on, gaining control of himself now that the revelation was over. "I'm still not sure it is real."

"It isn't real. You don't even like her." Andrew caught one fact in the whirling morass that was his brain and clung to it. "You've never said one good thing about her except that she had nice eyes."

"She has a spine, Andrew. I admire that about her."

"I've heard you call her pig-headed and lacking in knowledge of her place. Right here in this room, in fact."

It could not be true. James could not be engaged to

Claire. And she of all people would never have accepted him. She could barely stand to be in the same room, for heaven's sake!

"You must admit she is certainly both those things. But the fact remains, I have written to her mother declaring my intentions, and when I revealed this to Claire, she accepted my proposal."

"She couldn't have." Andrew couldn't make himself look beyond this. "She plans to become an engineer and—and explore the Amazon. Build airships. Construct bridges in China. Not become a peer's wife and serve tea to railroad presidents. No, James, you must be joking."

"I assure you I am not."

"The Claire I know would never marry you."

"Is that so?" James's tone had become dangerously soft. "And how well do you know her after less than a week?"

"I know she has ambitions. I know she cares for those children. I know she would never do this."

"And is it so bad, being engaged to me?"

Yes, it was. It was the worst thing that had ever happened. Because, Andrew now saw, if it were true, then she had chosen the wrong man.

If Claire Trevelyan was to marry anyone, it should be him.

Claire spent the next morning on the filing cabinets immediately behind Andrew's desk. Since everything that had been on the desk was presumably of current interest to him, it was logical to put it closer to hand. That meant, of course, that the contents of the first cabinet had to go somewhere. For now, she was making orderly piles on the floor.

Andrew had been very distracted earlier, giving her the barest greeting and then removing Tigg to the chamber to continue their experiments. Snouts, who had elected to stay outside and guard the landau, could be heard whistling now and again through the open window. At noon, Claire dusted off her hands and collected both boys for lunch.

"Where is Mr. Malvern?" she inquired of Tigg, pinning on her hat. "I've hardly spoken to him today."

"'E ent speakin' to anyone much, Lady. In a bit of a temper, 'e is. I left 'im in the back, fabricating another augmentation switch. Dunno as it'll do us much good, though. Electricks just ent made for this kind o' work."

"We shall see if our journey today will not change both his experiments and his temper. Come along."

After a fortifying lunch at a pub close to Tower Bridge, Claire piloted the landau south to St. George's Fields. There, she came to a halt outside the forbidding black iron bars of the fence that separated Bethlehem Royal Hospital from the sane world. Across the lawn and circular drive, the central cupola of the enormous institution rose above the fourth floor and into the sky. From somewhere they could hear the sound of birds twittering, and there were a few people pacing the lawn in quiet conversation. Other than that, there was no sound.

"If we go in there, we c'n come out again, right?"

Tigg said in a small voice.

"Even lunatics c'n 'ave visitors," Snouts said. "Buck up, mate."

A man came to the gate. "Your business?"

Claire raised her chin. "Lady Claire Craig, here to visit my cousin, Dr. Rosemary Craig, if you please."

"Certainly, milady." He unlocked the gate and Claire pushed the driving bar forward so that they rolled through. "You'll want to ask for her doctor in the receiving room, and they'll arrange to have her brought out."

"Thank you, sir." They progressed around the circular drive and came to a halt in front of the steps. Claire descended and removed her driving rig, then tugged her suit jacket into place and made sure her lace jabot was suitably fluffed. Then she noticed Tigg, who had not moved.

"Tigg? Aren't you coming?"

"Please, Lady," he whispered. "I can't do it. I can't go in there."

"Come on, Tigg," Snouts said in bracing tones. "I ent afraid, nor should you be."

From somewhere deep in the building came an ululating scream. Tigg flinched, and if he could have crept under the landau and laid flat upon the gravel, Claire was sure he would have. "Ent goin'," he whispered. "You can't make me."

"On second thought," Claire said, looking up at the doors, "I do not feel I should leave the landau unattended. Your logic is sound, Tigg. If you are willing to post a guard, I should be most grateful."

The boy drew a deep breath. "You c'n count on me, Lady." He slid out of the back and stood next to the passenger door, pressed against its gleaming surface as though glued there. "I shan't move from this spot, and no one shall touch this engine."

"Thank you, Tigg. You have set my mind at rest. Come along, Mr. McTavish. That silk cravat should be tucked into your waistcoat, not lying upon it. And don't forget to put on your spectacles."

So far today she had been two people: the Lady of Devices and the studious assistant to Andrew Malvern. Now Claire drew on a third persona—one oddly similar to that of her mother—like a cloak. She straightened her spine and tilted her chin so that she was obliged to look down her nose, and, grasping her skirts in one hand and her pocketbook containing her engineering notebook in the other, she sailed into the receiving room on a cloud of authority.

"I wish to visit my cousin, Dr. Rosemary Craig," she informed the nurse at the desk in pleasant, plummy tones. "I am Lady Claire Craig, of—of Craigsmoor House in Shropshire, and this is my secretary, Mr. McTavish."

The nurse looked awed, as though titled ladies did not come visiting so very often. Perhaps they did not. "Certainly, your ladyship. Let me fetch the doctor in charge of her case. In the meantime, perhaps you might care for some refreshment, here, in the sitting room?"

She showed them into a pleasant sitting room with white plaster walls and several chairs. In a moment she was back with a pitcher of water and three glasses, which she set on a side table. "The doctor will be with you shortly."

Claire had just poured herself and Snouts a glass of water when a man in a white coat came in. He looked very much like the dreadful person at the British Museum who had interviewed her for a position—and been much more interested in her anatomy than in her knowledge of cataloguing specimens. Claire forced down her instant, irrational distaste and extended a hand.

"Lady Claire," he said politely, shaking it. "I am Doctor Thomas Longmont, at your service."

"How do you do? This is my secretary, Mr. McTavish." Snouts shook hands gravely, his spectacles winking in the light from the front window.

"I understand you wish to see your cousin, Rosemary Craig. You will no doubt be very welcome, but first, I feel I should prepare you, since this is your first visit here."

"Prepare me, sir? Is Rosemary not well?" She bit her lip. Of course she was not well. That was why she was locked up in here. "I mean—"

He smiled. "I imagine you meant is she suffering from an illness other than that of the mind. Let me assure you, in body she is sound. However, in mind ... How long has it been since you last saw your cousin?"

Claire pretended to consider. "I was a child, and she and her family—my aunt and uncle, and cousin Dorothy—had come to Craigmoor House for Christmas. I believe she had just made a grand presentation to the Royal Society of Engineers, so it was a very merry holiday for all of us."

Snouts gazed at her in admiration for this feat of storytelling. Claire ignored him and fixed a pleasant expression on her face as she waited for the doctor to speak.

"So it has been some years, then. Well, let me tell you briefly of her condition, which I hope will not cause you too much distress." He tugged on his pant legs and seated himself. "Her affect is disconcerting. Be prepared for that at first. She cannot look anyone in the eye, and her replies to questions make no sense. She persists in believing her family are the mad ones, and she is perfectly sane, so I beg you, do not let your natural compassion and feminine sympathy overcome good sense." He paused, as if gathering himself for the worst. "The presence of your secretary is fraught with danger, I am afraid. She has an intense dislike of men, even those who, like myself, are acting in her best interests. At the same time, she has a history of violence, so the presence of this young man with you is a positive. All I can do is post an orderly within calling distance, who will be ready to intervene at the slightest sign from you."

Claire was sure she had gone pale, and indeed, the doctor searched her face.

"You may well be shocked. Miss Craig is not the same woman you remember from happier times in the bosom of the family, I am very sorry to say."

She nodded, and rose on unsteady knees. "May I see her now?"

HER OWN DEVICES

9

Dr. Longmont led them out. "The incurables are housed in their own wing, with their own airing garden. It would not do to mix them with the patients undergoing more successful methods of treatment."

Claire felt Snouts close beside her, and indeed, felt no embarrassment at all in taking his arm and gripping it. They proceeded down a long gallery lined with doors. This was clearly the women's side, and female patients in various states of dress and dishevelment walked up and down ... or sat, drooping, by the windows. Or, in one case, lay on the floor in a corner, sobbing uncontrollably. From inside a room came that same throbbing scream that had so frightened Tigg, and Claire distinctly felt Snouts flinch.

SHELLEY ADINA

They turned right and proceeded past a pair of double doors marked COLD BATHS and another marked ELECTRICK THERAPY.

Claire looked away.

The doctor unlocked a set of doors with the key that hung in a small cabinet bearing a combination lock, and they were in the incurables wing. This corridor was much shorter, and every door was closed and locked. Claire could see people's heads through small windows in the doors—people in constant motion, it seemed, flying at the walls, walking in circles, gawking at the visitors, mouths open.

They passed through another door and moved through the ward, with beds against the walls, presumably for less dangerous incurables. An orderly in a clean white uniform joined them. Claire glanced at the beds. At top and bottom were leather straps, the kind that might wrap around ankle or wrist. Another set of locked doors, and then they were outside.

A deep breath did nothing to clear the miasma of fear and distress flowing out the door behind them.

The airing garden was a square of lawn with a couple of stone benches. At the far end, a woman in a white dressing gown sat, staring fixedly at a stone wall the height of two men. No one else appeared to be taking the air today, though the afternoon was fine.

"Remember," Dr. Longmont said, "at the slightest sign of agitation, Mr. Wellburn here will be at hand to help."

"Thank you," Claire whispered.

"Would you like me to go with you?"

She would like him to take her back through all those locked doors to the main entrance, so she could escape this place. "No, thank you. She will remember me, I am sure."

He nodded, and left them. Claire took a deep breath and she and Snouts approached the figure in white. An attempt had been made to dress her hair, but without hairpins it was difficult to do much more than braid it. Her posture was rigidly straight, as though she still wore a corset.

"Doctor Craig?" No response. Claire circled around to stand before her. "Doctor Craig, I am Lady Claire Trevelyan, daughter of Viscount St. Ives. I am posing as your cousin from Shropshire in order to visit you."

A tremor seemed to run through the woman's body, but her gaze remained fixed on a point at the top of the wall.

Well, she was not deaf. Claire saw no choice but to sit next to her and proceed. "I do hope you will not reveal my deception to the worthy doctor. The reason for my visit is that I believe I am in possession of one of your lightning devices. Contrary to popular belief, not all of them seem to have been destroyed. I have come today in hopes that you might be able to educate me on how they work."

"Work equals force times displacement," the lady murmured.

Snouts shifted his weight, and Dr. Craig's head whipped around at the movement. She drew in a startled breath.

"This is my secretary, Mr. McTavish," Claire said

SHELLEY ADINA

quickly, before the outrage on the woman's face could resolve itself into something else—a scream, perhaps, or physical violence. "He means you no harm. He is here for moral support. I—I have never visited Bedlam before."

Exhaling, the woman focused on a point over Claire's knee.

This was hopeless. If she did not react at the mention of her devices, the destruction of which had brought her to this place, then had she forgotten them? Had the trip out here been for nothing?

She studied the woman's face, and realized she was not gazing into space, but was in fact focused on her pocketbook, and more specifically, on the shape of the notebook within.

Work equals force times displacement. A physics formula.

Claire drew it out, along with a pencil. "This is my engineering notebook," she said. "I've been keeping a record of the devices I've made—not on the scale of yours, of course. My aspirations and talent are much more modest." She opened the book and paged through it. "This is a gaseous capsaicin bomb, and here are sketches for my firelamps, recently used with much success. I was quite pleased with the magnetic steering mechanisms, here."

Ah. She had the scientist's attention. Gone was the unfocused gaze and instead, Claire saw the intensity of someone whose concentration was absolute. She turned a page. "This is a sketch of an augmentation assembly for elec—"

* 86 *

HER OWN DEVICES

A bony white finger came down on the page. "That cell is not nearly powerful enough."

Claire gained control of her face and proceeded as if they had been conversing all along. "I know. It's most distressing. The chamber has at least three augmentation assemblies and none of them seem to be able to produce enough power."

"What are you trying to accomplish?"

"My employer wants to increase the carbon density of coal so that it will burn longer, reducing the cost of long-distance travel by train."

"Lunkheads." The lady's mouth pursed. She took the book away from Claire entirely, and waggled her fingers impatiently for the pencil. Then she began to draw, the precise, perfectly curved strokes of someone who lives and breathes engineering. "You can't augment city electrics, or draw extra current without endangering the entire system. You have to start fresh." On the paper, a chamber began to take shape. "You don't use electricks. You use kineticks."

"As the mother's helpers do?" Claire had briefly considered this, but the cell would need to be huge in order to power the chamber, so she had discarded the idea.

"It is similar, but not quite. With it, you could treat your coal in a conductive chamber." She laid the pencil down and pushed the book onto Claire's lap.

"This is similar to what he has in place. But the cell is what is stumping us. The one I have is this big—" Claire held her gloved fingers two inches apart. "—which I am quite certain would be inadequate."

Dr. Craig gazed at her. "Where did you get it?"

"It was built into a rifle by a man called Luke Jackson, who turned from engineering to a life of crime. I call it the lightning rifle."

"It can kill a man, you know."

"Yes, I know." Claire's own gaze did not falter. "I need you to tell me how to construct a similar cell that might power this chamber."

"Without burning down half of London? Why should I do that?" The anger, which had been temporarily held back by the dam of intellectual inquiry, flooded into her face. "Why should I help you, a perfect stranger, when no one will help me?"

"You have no reason in the world to do so," Claire said steadily. "But if even one small part of your legacy still exists, and I can prove it works, would not that go some way to repairing your reputation—if not your situation here?"

Dr. Craig whirled on the seat to face Claire directly. "Do you think I'm mad?" she demanded.

"I have no idea. Are you?"

"Certainly not. And yet here I am, disintegrating year after year until even I begin to doubt myself."

"The doctor and your sister both said you would say that."

"Of course they did. And do you know why, young lady?"

Claire shook her head. She was no longer frightened, but all the same, her body tensed in case she needed to flee.

"Thomas Longmont is the younger brother of

HER OWN DEVICES

George Longmont, whose name I presume you have heard?" At Claire's nod, she went on, "George saw the promise—the genius—in my work and realized the effect it would have on the family. The Longmont men have a monopoly on the board of directors of the London Electrick Company—and a commensurate monopoly on the stock."

Claire took a breath as the enormity of the case suddenly became clear. Her back relaxed against the bench as the tension went out of her. "Your invention could revolutionize electricks. It could even put the LEC out of business."

"So instead of embracing the new and changing the old to keep up with the times, they destroyed every example of my work and had me committed—with the collusion of my sister, who is a vindictive, jealous woman." Her face turned bleak. "Much to my sorrow."

"And yet she visits you every month," Claire said in tones of wonder. How could such a Machiavellian plot be permitted to take place in this modern day and age?

"She does not visit me. I believe she has designs on Doctor Longmont, poor girl. She listens to his report on my 'progress' and simpers and smiles and goes away satisfied with her charity. And they say *I'm* mad. Thomas Longmont will never marry her. He much prefers the company of gentlemen, all of them smoking cigars and playing cards and ruling the world from the comfort of their club."

"How do you know all this?"

"Everyone knows everything about the staff here. And about each other. For all the good it does us."

Claire had never seen a lunatic, but this woman did not seem mad in the least. Angry, yes—perhaps debilitatingly so—but not insane. Her faculties seemed to be as sharp as ever, and if what she said was true, she had been dealt a criminal injustice.

One that deserved reparation.

But it could not be fought through the courts—young as she was, even Claire could see that a collusion of powerful men would never allow the case to see daylight.

Therefore, the solution must come during the night.

"Doctor Craig, how tall is that wall?"

"Fifteen feet, five and three-quarter inches. Not including the iron spikes."

"And what are the security measures in this facility?"

"Here in the incurables wing, we are locked in and let out only for meals, for physical examination, and for therapy." The emphasis on this last word came as bitter as acid. "Those of us considered less of a danger to ourselves and others have a bed on the ward, but we are strapped down at night. The ward is likewise locked. Their electricks room is a travesty, used for torture, not healing, and I do not wish to discuss the use of the cold baths." She mastered herself, and went on in a calmer tone. "This is the first time I have been in the airing garden in six months. I have been amusing myself by triangulating the height of the wall."

"Is there a guard on duty?"

"No guards, only the orderlies. But you have no doubt noticed they are hired less for their medical knowledge and more for the beefiness of their physiques."

HER OWN DEVICES

"You say you are among those on the ward?" Tied down to the bed to sleep. Dear heaven. "What kind of lock does it possess?"

"A bolt only, on the outside. Getting into the wing itself from the main hospital is more difficult. It requires the combination to the key cabinet, which is a closely guarded secret. What do you propose, young lady?"

Claire hitched herself a little closer to the woman on the bench. "I propose that in exchange for releasing you from this prison, you build a kinetick cell for my employer. Once that is complete, we will have no further obligation to one another and you will be free to take up your life again in whatever manner you please."

A flicker of amusement creased Dr. Craig's face, brief as lightning. "And how do you plan to keep your side of the bargain?"

Over the lady's shoulder, Claire saw the orderly walking toward them. Beefy he was, to be sure. And her hour was up. "I must go. Tonight, at three o'clock, be prepared to leave."

Claire rose and smiled at the orderly. He offered her his arm, and as they paced away across the lawn, she glanced back.

Dr. Rosemary Craig had approached the wall and appeared to be counting the bricks, her fingers investigating each seam and crack.

It would seem the scientist was preparing already.

10

"'Ow you plannin' to pull this off, Lady?" Snouts inquired when they were safely back in the landau and bowling down Lambeth Road.

"Never mind 'ow, what about why?" Tigg wanted to know, his chocolate eyes huge. "Releasin' lunatics? Wiv respect, Lady, are you mad?"

"I am not, and neither is she." Claire made the turn just before the bridge and headed upriver for the cottage. "If Mr. Malvern is to succeed, we need her knowledge, because it seems all of our brains together are not sufficient for the task. I am convinced the lightning cell is the key to making his chamber work."

"So, wot then ... you'll just turn up in the laboratory wiv a mad scientist and Mr. Malvern'll stand aside while she does as she pleases?"

Claire collected her thoughts while she negotiated another turn, then pushed the bar out until they were traveling at a refreshing thirty miles per hour away from St. George's Fields. "We have two options, Tigg. Either we bring her into the lab and introduce her, or we fabricate the cell in the privacy of our own cottage and present it as a *fait accompli.*"

"I dunno wot that is, but if you mean passin' it off as if we done it, that don't seem right, either."

"You are quite correct. So, it appears as if we must go with the first option and present the lady herself." She was not yet sure how she would manage that, but one thing at a time.

The boys remained quiet for the rest of the journey. It wasn't until they had rolled to a stop outside the cottage that Snouts said, "So at t'risk of repeatin' meself, 'ow we gonna do this, then?"

"Come inside," Claire said, gathering her things—including the lightning rifle from under the seat. "This is going to be rather ... complicated. I am going to need every man Jack of you if we are to complete our preparations before midnight."

Their single greatest advantage was that the walls of Bedlam were meant to keep people in, not out. In fact, Claire reflected as she secured a loop in the rope to the brass clip on her leather corselet, this was probably the first time in recorded history that anyone had tried to break in.

Her black skirts were secured above her knees, revealing only black woolen stockings, and the lightning rifle's comforting weight rested on her back. A black gauze scarf would conceal her features, though at the moment it was wrapped around her shoulders.

The wall, though smooth and relatively featureless on the inside, was easy enough to scale on the outside. A barrel and a damaged crate got them halfway up, and the grappling hook and rope took care of the rest.

The airing garden had no illumination of any kind—only the glow of the electricks in the corridors shone through the glass, which was not enough to cause any difficulty. The long shadow of the building would provide cover once they could reach it. A night bird twittered some distance away down the street toward the corner of Lambeth Road.

Lizzie, standing watch.

"Quickly," Claire whispered. "Someone's coming—probably the bobbies."

She tugged on her rope, and on the other side of the wall, Snouts hauled on his end. Up she went, her corselet creaking as it took her weight, her feet in their sturdy boots scrambling for purchase. At the top, she pulled herself upright using the iron spikes, thankful that Bedlam had not yet seen the necessity for embedding broken glass in their masonry.

She slid down the inner side, and when Snouts caught her, released the rope from its clip. They had no choice but to leave it hanging there, ready for the return trip. She heard the scrape of boots on cobbles on the other side as her team scattered into the streets and alleys opposite, and then silence. The air sawed in and out of her lungs as she tried to breathe quietly, huddled with Snouts behind the bench she had occupied that afternoon.

A pair of male voices murmured, and they distinctly heard the scrape of the barrel as the bobbies—if that was who they were—disassembled their makeshift ramp.

Please don't let them look up and see the hook.

A very long ten minutes later, another night bird called at the opposite end of the block. Maggie, sounding the all clear.

"It's all right," Snouts whispered. "We can manage wivout a stair."

"I hope Doctor Craig can, too. Come."

Keeping close to the ground, they dashed across the open lawn and into the shadows. Claire moved along the wall of the incurables wing, Snouts close behind her, until they reached a set of frosted glass windows. "The cold baths," she whispered. "This is the easiest way in, and the furthest from anyone with ears."

Snouts gazed upward. "Lady, they got bars on 'em. You proposin' to squeeze between?"

"No, I'm proposing to use the rifle."

She unholstered it and pushed the switch. The hum sounded uncomfortably loud in the silence, but instead of allowing the charge to build up to lethal force, she stepped back and took aim at the window. If one sent a bolt of power into sand, the result was glass. And if one sent a bolt of power into glass ...

A tendril of blue-white light arced across the space,

illuminating every leaf in the shrubbery before spreading over the surface of the window like spidery cracks in a sheet of ice. With a shivering sound, the window disintegrated into a million shards, sifting into piles of glittering grains on the sill.

"Completely disintegrated and returned to sand," Claire whispered. "One would think it would melt, but no. It's a property of this current that—"

"Lady! C'n we leave the lesson for after?"

Right. Perhaps after Dr. Craig was vindicated in the eyes of her peers, Claire would write a paper on the properties of the current. Leaving out its uses for burglary and vandalism, of course.

Meanwhile, the iron bars still remained.

Another dose of the current took care of this problem, as the metal glowed, cracked, and fell into the shrubbery like a house of cards falling down, no matter how hard Snouts tried to catch them in his gloved hands. The noise was deafening.

They dropped to their knees, frozen in place. Another long ten minutes went by, but when the sleeping building did not rouse with an alarm, Claire gripped the sill and hoisted herself in.

She did not need to tell Snouts to exercise caution. He was taut with nerves, his face a pale mask. She was rather tense herself, as she skirted the dual tanks of water. They were not bathing pools, exactly, bearing no resemblance to those in the gymnasium at St. Cecelia's. They were big enough to accommodate perhaps two people, floating, and from the light seeping in through the window in the door, seemed about five feet deep.

HER OWN DEVICES

Dr. Craig had not wanted to speak of them.

The sound of their footsteps echoed off the water in an uncanny way. Claire made her way to the door as quickly as she could. She was quite prepared to shoot it, but it was not locked. Evidently the main doors to the incurables' wing kept the general populace out, and the baths themselves kept the incurables out.

Unless they were brought here under duress.

They slipped through and around the corner to the doors to the ward. The bolt slid across easily, and, knees bent so they could not be seen by a sleepless lunatic through the locked rooms' little windows, they crept into the ward.

Which bed belonged to Dr. Craig?

Claire berated herself for not finding out. They had not been occupied this afternoon, and she had been so horrified by the leather straps that she had put the entire ward out of her mind. Now she must pay for that mistake.

"Stand guard," she whispered in Snouts's ear. As silently as she could, she glided down the aisle between the beds. It was impossible to see. The light filtering through the ward door was not enough to make out the features of the sleeping women, and she dared not switch on the electricks overhead.

At least, she hoped the women were sleeping.

Someone made a sound practically under her feet, and Claire jumped, clapping a hand to her lips just in time to muffle her own cry.

"Mama?" a woman said. "Papa's hurting me." Claire moved to the next bed. "Mama?" the woman said, louder.

Oh dear. Someone would come, and there was nowhere but the lockers at the end of the ward to hide. And once they were hidden, how would they get out? These walls were designed to contain, and designed well.

"Shh, dear," she whispered. "You're all right."

"But he's hurting me. Make him stop."

"I shall. Mama will shoot him and then he won't hurt you any more."

The woman seemed to subside. Claire fervently hoped that her dreams would not come up in discussion with her doctor.

"Who's there?" came a voice at the far end of the ward. "Is that you?"

Swiftly, Claire moved toward the sound. "Doctor Craig?" she whispered.

"Of course. I've been awake all night. You'll have to undo these straps."

They were tighter than Claire expected. How did the doctors think the women were going to sleep, battened down like this? She unfastened the buckles by feel—one hand, one foot, then the reverse on the other side. Dr. Craig gathered the thin woolen blanket around her shoulders and swung her legs over the iron bedstead.

"Where are your clothes?"

"I have none," she whispered back. "They were all confiscated when I was admitted. I have nothing but this nightdress and blanket."

"Possessions?"

"None."

"Money?"

"Of course not."

"Right, then. Let's go."

"Mama?" Blast, the woman had awakened again. "Mama, make him stop."

"I will, dear," Claire whispered as she went past.

"Don't encourage her," snapped Dr. Craig. "It makes the memories more intense and upsets her."

"Mama!" The woman was struggling against her restraints now. "Mama!"

Botheration. Snouts held the door and they hurried through, then locked it behind them. "This way!"

"Papa, no!" They heard the terrified shriek through the solid wood panel, and Claire skidded around the corner and pushed open the door to the cold baths.

"What are you doing? I'm not going in there!"

"Afraid you are, ma'am," Snouts said behind her.

"Take your hands off me!"

He pushed her through and closed the door behind him. Now the woman on the ward was screaming, and down the corridor, they could hear the approach of running feet.

"Doctor Craig, you must go through the window. Stop this struggling at once!" Claire grabbed her hand and between the two of them, they dragged the woman around the two tanks and over to the window, where Claire jumped down and Snouts pushed her out.

"Oof!" Dr. Craig fell heavily on her hands and knees.

"They'll have seen you're missing by now."

Dr. Craig dragged in a shaky breath. "I ... hate ..."

"I know. Come. We haven't much time."

Running low, the three of them dashed across the lawn. Snouts whistled and tugged on the rope to be sure the grappling hook still held. An answering whistle came from the other side. Still clear.

"I'll take you up pick-a-back, ma'am," Snouts said tersely, bending his knees. Without giving her a chance to protest, Claire boosted her onto his back. Fortunately, the scientist was not a hefty woman. Snouts gripped the rope and began to climb while Claire watched frantically over her shoulder.

The longest thirty seconds of her life passed, while Snouts grunted and scraped his way up the rope and onto the top of the wall. From there, he delivered Dr. Craig into unseen hands and at last it was Claire's turn.

She had never gone up a rope so fast. She had just stepped over the iron spikes when a shout from the building—outside the building—brought her head up.

"Oy! You there! Stop!" A man ran across the lawn, his white coat flapping around his knees.

Claire didn't wait to see any more. She gripped the rope and leaped, the rough hemp burning through her gloved hands so fast she could feel its heat. She landed in the street with a thump.

"Leave the hook," she gasped. "Billy Bolt!"

The hem of Dr. Craig's night robe vanished into a dark alley, and Claire dove across the street to follow it. Dodging from one building to the next, it wasn't until two streets over that she could open up and run in earnest.

The silky gleam of the landau waiting on the corner of the next road, with Tigg in the driving seat, was as welcome as a sunrise.

HER OWN DEVICES

By the time the Southwark bobbies had been roused and begun to comb the area for the escaped lunatic, Dr. Craig was being ushered into the cottage in Vauxhall Gardens—disheveled, out of breath, and still struggling to believe that the evidence of her senses was actually the truth.

She had been broken out of Bedlam and was free for the first time in over a decade.

11

The first order of business was to find clothes for their guest, since one could not go about in a nightdress, particularly in a house full of boys. Claire had just tied Maggie's blue hair bow—the one that went with her best dress—in preparation for a shopping trip to Regent Street, when she heard the familiar whoosh and thump of a tube arriving.

Dear Lady Claire,

May I offer my greetings and best wishes for your continued good health. I am in receipt of your letter inquiring after the property adjacent to the Regent Bridge and am happy to tell you that it belongs to a business entity whose directors assure me they are only too happy to sell. Having taken a drive to inspect said property, I confess myself mystified as to your reasons for the purchase. However, your business is your own and I would not presume to interfere.

I recommend that you offer no more than fifty pounds sterling for the place—a sum so generous, considering its condition and present occupants, that I am sure you will not need to negotiate further. If you agree, I will begin proceedings immediately. Once you have the deed in hand, you will need to hire bully-boys to turn out the squatters that appear to be living there at present. I know a man who could handle this for you.

I have heard interesting rumors that the glassworks on the other side of the bridge is looking to establish a housing development for its workers. Should this prove to be the case, you stand to make a tidy profit when they make you an offer for the property. I would be happy to act on your behalf in that event.

Yours truly,
Richard Arundel
Arundel & Hollis, Solicitors

Excellent. Claire folded up the letter and tucked it into her reticule for answer later. It was clear the good Mr. Arundel did not pay much attention to the address codes on his tubes—which was all to the good. He would be terribly embarrassed had he known he had referred to her as a squatter.

"Will you be comfortable here until I come back?" she asked Dr. Craig, who was sitting on the bed attempting to make Weepin' Willie answer her questions.

"Yes, certainly, once I find some breakfast. I haven't had such an appetite in years. Why will this child not speak?"

"'E don't," Lizzie said, ever brief and to the point.

"Is he dumb?"

"'E ent."

"Is he damaged psychologically?"

"Hey, now, don't be sayin' such about our Willie." Lizzie's frown was fearsome. "Lunatics wot got sprung out o' Bedlam got no right to call others names."

Claire gasped. "Lizzie! Apologize to Dr. Craig at once."

"She 'as to go first."

To Claire's surprise, Dr. Craig was not offended—or even shocked. "My dear child, *psychological* simply means dealing with the mind. Sometimes a trauma early in one's life can produce effects such as the inability to speak. I simply wondered if this was the case with, er, Willie."

Lizzie eyed her, unconvinced.

"And I am not a lunatic," Dr. Craig went on in the same tone. "I was put in Bethlehem Royal Hospital against my will by powerful men who wished to keep me quiet."

"About what?"

"About my devices, among other things."

"You gonna teach the Lady 'ow to make 'em?"

HER OWN DEVICES

"That is our agreement. And I would very much like to begin work, so if you are joining Lady Claire in her expedition to find me clothes, I offer my thanks and wish you good speed."

Lizzie hovered by the door. "Sorry I called yer a lunatic, Doc."

"That is quite all right. You were laboring under a misapprehension, easily corrected."

Claire went downstairs, hoping her astonishment was not plain on her face. Lizzie had never apologized to anyone in all the weeks they had been acquainted. She had come close to it once, but the words had not actually crossed her lips.

Perhaps the child was becoming civilized after all.

In Regent Street, Claire purchased a corset, several sets of unmentionables, a good walking skirt in navy wool, and two blouses of the sort she herself favored. Last, at the expedition outfitters' in Market Street, she bought boots, a duster, and goggles so that the scientist's clothes would not be damaged from traveling in the landau—or anywhere else.

"Is the Doc goin' to South America?" Maggie gazed at the parcels and bags in wonder.

"She may, someday, as may we all," Claire answered, stowing everything in the compartment behind the seat. "But for now, she may ride with us safely. What do you say to some tea at Fortnum's and some new boots for the two of you?"

When they were comfortably seated in the tea room and had each ordered a plate of finger sandwiches, she looked up from enjoying her own creamed soup to see

Emilie Fragonard across the room.

Her best friend from her past life was enjoying tea with a party of girls Claire vaguely remembered from their class at school. How strange. She hadn't realized Emilie had been close with anyone but herself. But how lovely to see her here. She put down her spoon.

"Stay here and enjoy your lunch, girls. I'm just going over there by that row of potted palms to say hello to the young lady in the yellow sprigged walking dress."

"'Ave a sandwich." Maggie pointed to a delicacy on her plate. "These little 'uns with crab inside are ever so good."

Maggie was right. The crab sandwiches were indeed delicious. Claire could empathize with Dr. Craig in one way, at least—food never tasted so good until you had gone a long time without any. She would never take it for granted again.

She made her way between the tables, glad she'd dressed in a particularly nice waist with eyelet embroidery and rows of tucking, and that—thank you, Cowboy Poker—her hat was new, pleated at the back and trimmed with a jaunty blue-and-white striped bow. "Emilie! I'm so glad to see you."

The astonishment in her friend's eyes behind their spectacles was almost comical. "Claire! Oh, Claire, whatever happened to you? Are you mad?" Emilie gathered her into a hug that was so sympathetic it almost hurt. "Dearest, to what desperate straits you have been driven—and to think I am partly responsible!"

Claire righted her hat and sank into the nearest gilded chair. "I—what?" She directed a vague smile at the other two girls. What were their names? And what on earth was Emilie talking about?

"We have just heard the news, haven't we?" Emilie appealed to the others, who nodded. "About your engagement to Lord James Selwyn. It's all over London. Claire, you don't even like him!"

Oh. That.

Claire gathered her wits. She had been so focused on electricks and in freeing Dr. Craig that she had not devoted a single thought to her new fiancé, nor thought up an appropriate story to explain him.

"He—he has improved on further acquaintance," she said rather lamely.

"I heard he was a shocking rogue," said the girl on the left in a voice just above a whisper. "And that no lady is safe with him."

"Abigail, that can't be true," the other girl said. "Claire would never engage herself to a man like that."

Abigail. Yes. That meant the other one had to be Charlotte. They were cousins, but for the life of her, Claire couldn't remember their surnames. "Certainly not," she said. "I feel perfectly safe with him." As long as she had her lightning rifle to hand.

"You shall be Baroness Selwyn," sighed Abigail. "A perfect match, since you are the daughter of a viscount."

"The sister of one, presently," Emilie corrected her. "Claire, do tell us how this came about."

Oh, dear. "He wrote to my mother informing her of his intentions, and then he proposed."

"Oh, you comical person. But was it terribly romantic?" Charlotte wanted to know. "Was it outdoors, in a pavilion, or indoors, with a bouquet of flowers?"

Flowers. Paper. In the hearth. "Indoors, with flowers."

Charlotte clasped her hands in delight and subsided.

"So you will be comfortably situated and I can stop worrying," Emilie said. "I take it you are with your grand-aunts Beaton in Greenwich?"

"No indeed." So Emilie's mother was still monitoring her correspondence, and she had not received Claire's tube sent days and days ago. "I wrote to you some time ago to let you know my situation. Perhaps I miscoded the tube." She smiled for the cousins' benefit, while Emilie's smile faded and her lips thinned. "I am employed as assistant to a scientist, and am supervising the education of a number of young persons." She nodded toward the Mopsies, who were signaling the waiter with imperious energy. "Two of the girls are over there, by the window."

"They look delightful," said Abigail. "What pretty dresses. Who are they?"

"Orphans. They are, however, very intelligent and their lessons are coming along briskly."

"Fancy you a teacher," Abigail said. "I never would have guessed."

"Claire has always done well in school," Emilie said loyally. "I wouldn't have passed Mathematics were it not for her."

"What I meant was, with the Arabian Bubble and everything ... well, let's just say it's quite a surprise you're the first of our class to be engaged. And don't think that hasn't frosted Lady Julia's turned-up nose."

Abigail's smile was triumphant, as if she had produced a baron herself. "I hear she actually threw china."

"Lady Julia is far too well bred for that," Claire said. Though she could certainly believe it.

"Maybe she wanted Lord James for herself," Abigail mused.

"If she wanted him for anyone, it was for Gloria Meriwether-Astor. That girl is looking for a title to go with all her father's money, and Julia made no secret out of how amusing it would be to find one for her."

"I'm sure the gentlemen appreciated that," Emilie sniffed. "What are they, Bengal tigers to be bagged and mounted?"

This produced a round of giggling, and Claire felt herself flush as heads turned toward them. "I must be getting back to my charges before they order everything on the menu. Emilie, I trust I may write?" *You must get to the mail before your mother does.*

"Yes, do." *Never fear, now that I know what she's been up to.* "I hope I may come and call?" *Don't visit our house, though. She'll toss you out just as she did before.*

"My situation doesn't allow it, but I would love to meet for tea. I must attend my duties at the laboratory in the mornings, but I am free in the afternoons." *Please don't deny me your friendship. I could not bear it.*

"I shall look forward to it." *Never. We are friends forever.*

When she got back to her table, the Mopsies were digging into a plum trifle, one on either side of it.

"D'you think Granny Protheroe could make summat like this, Lady?"

It took a moment for Claire to cross the gauzy border between old life and new. Granny Protheroe. The cottage. Yes.

She arranged her skirts and addressed herself once more to her soup. "I'm sure she could. People can surprise you with what they know."

So the news of her engagement was out. She had not said a word, so James must have taken it upon himself to announce it. And since Emilie did not move in his circles, it must indeed be all over London if it had filtered down to her.

Well, she had accepted James's proposal knowing that this could work to her advantage. What she had not expected was how trapped it would make her feel.

"The boots are a touch on the large side, but no matter." Dr. Craig tried to see more of herself than the single cracked mirror in Claire's room would allow. "I shall wear thicker stockings. You have a good eye for fit."

"Now that you can go about, you can exchange them," Claire replied. She did have rather a good eye. The skirt could have been made to order. There was even a little room for the scientist to gain some weight.

"I shall not waste my time on boots when I have a debt to pay." Dr. Craig abandoned the mirror. "Shall we begin?"

"I am taking the children to church this morning, but we may certainly begin this afternoon. Then tomorrow morning I shall introduce you to Mr. Malvern, my employer."

"I have given some thought to your awkward position. I shall merely say that I have been released, and in the interests of science offer my modest talents to his venture."

"Do you think he will believe it?" Claire couldn't help but think that the coincidence of timing might be considered suspicious.

"From what you have told me, I think he is becoming desperate at his inability to harness electricks for his purposes. Expediency will overcome suspicion, you may depend upon it."

Claire rounded up the Mopsies—giving them strict instructions that on no account were Sunday pockets to be picked—and Willie. Jake was lounging on the porch overlooking the river when they emerged.

When he got up as if he intended to come with them, Claire tried to hide her astonishment. "Are you joining us this morning?"

"Snouts gave orders one of us ought to go with you anytime yer out."

"But it's Sunday morning, Jake. I am hardly likely to be set upon at St. Peter's. And we were out most of yesterday without protection."

"Snouts, 'e's nervous since ye sprung th' Doc. Figures she'll draw attention we don't want."

Claire gave up. "Very well. Since we are walking, I suppose he is quite right." And perhaps an hour in church would be good for Jake, though the good Lord had His work cut out for Him there.

The Mopsies weren't happy about giving up a morning's work on the walking coop, wriggling and whispering to distraction, but Willie was quiet in the pew beside her, gazing up at the ceiling and examining the carvings. And to her enormous surprise, he attempted to sing during the hymns.

The Mopsies gawked, and even Jake looked amazed. "Willie, you can so speak!" Maggie whispered, elbowing him. "Why don't you say anyfink at the cottage?"

But silence claimed him once again, and throughout the service, Claire wondered if Dr. Craig could be right. Had something happened in his early years that had deprived him of the will, but not the ability? And how would one ever find out, since he did not answer any question put to him using words, no matter what the subject?

After lunch, she put this puzzle aside in favor of another one. She fetched the lightning rifle and handed it to Dr. Craig, who took it in both hands with care, as if it might explode, and examined it minutely. "I see," she murmured. "No finesse, but it is obviously operable." She looked up. "I am surprised you have not reverse engineered it and duplicated the device yourself."

"I would have, had I not feared I could not put it back together again. The connections are straightforward, but the device itself ... since there is only one in existence, I did not want to risk it."

With fingers that were hesitant at first, then more confident, the scientist began to disassemble the rifle.

Claire clamped her lips shut on a protest. If the inventor of the device could not reassemble it, then no one could.

"There, you see?" Dr. Craig held up the cell. "Released from its servitude. Now, let me show you how it works."

"I am most interested in how it converts elec—"

"Oh, no." Dr. Craig had the brass cover off. "It's not electricks. It uses kineticks."

"I know, but there must be some conversion process that—"

"No. See?" She laid the pieces on the worktable, each tiny gear and bit of clockwork placed in order. "You understand how lightning is created in the natural universe?"

Lewis, who had been leaning over to watch, recited what Claire had taught them verbatim. Jake elbowed him none too gently in the ribs. "Clever-clogs, stop showin' off."

"Think of this device as a miniature heaven. Kineticks move the particles, which build up the charge, which causes the rifle to fire the bolt."

The assembly fell into place in Claire's head. "That's what is wrong with Mr. Malvern's chamber." She locked eyes with Tigg across the table. "He is trying to apply electricks to the coal when what he should be doing is creating a charge in the chamber, the same way it is created in this device."

Tigg wasted no words, simply fetched a bit of brown paper and a pencil from her case. Claire sketched the changes that would be needed in the chamber. "We can bring this to him tomorrow. That way, Dr. Craig's visit can be shortened to the absolute minimum necessary for politeness. His laboratory is too close to St. George's Fields for my comfort."

"I quite agree with you," the scientist said. "Now, my dear, if you would reassemble this device for me? I shall watch in case you take a wrong turn."

On her third attempt, which involved using a toothpick as a tiny screwdriver, the scientist nodded. "You'll do. Now, mount it in the rifle."

This was much easier. Claire had it back together in seconds.

"Excellent. Now, take the rifle apart again and put it back together—blindfolded."

Tigg let out a yelp of laughter as Claire allowed Maggie to tie her sash over her eyes. It was difficult, but the workings were laid out in her head. She would be able to assemble the rifle in the dark.

How odd that the scientist had thought it right for her to prepare for such a thing.

When she was finished, she pinned Tigg in place with a glance. "Your turn." The smile fell from his face. Smugly, she tied the blindfold on him herself.

HER OWN DEVICES

12

Dr. Craig enjoyed her second trip in the steam landau much more than she had her first. "This is such a novelty," she called over the wind, holding her borrowed chiffon scarf in place under her chin with one hand. "Even at his most successful, my father could never have afforded one. He was a horse and carriage man, in any case."

"It is all I have left of my father," Claire confessed, watching the road. "He was a forward thinker." It was such a pity he had not applied his thinking in the right direction. It still hurt, deep inside, knowing he had gambled the safety of his family and the futures of his children on something as frivolous as the combustion engine. Were they not worth more to him?

In the end, however, even life was not. Only she and her mother knew he had taken his own life in despair when the Arabian Bubble burst.

At the laboratory, Dr. Craig and Tigg climbed out while Claire shut the engine down. And then the awkward moment that she had dreaded was at hand.

Andrew Malvern stood by the cold chamber, gazing at it disconsolately. He had not even put on his leather apron yet, and he hunched into his frock coat, though the morning was pleasant.

He would not have believed it was possible to be so miserable. Not only was he out of ideas, he was actually considering smashing the chamber to bits, dissolving his partnership, and offering his services as a mechanic on an airship to Australia.

He might just do it, too. If Claire was going to be James's wife, he didn't want to be here to watch.

The familiar singing sputter of the landau came down Orpington Close, and he braced himself to see her.

"Mr. Malvern," she called when the door opened, "we have a guest this morning."

James, probably. Though he was no guest. Still, there was no way on this earth he would allow James to see how much his engagement had hurt him. So he struggled to shrug off his blue devils and don civility like another garment.

"Dr. Rosemary Craig, may I present Mr. Andrew Malvern, of the Royal Society of Engineers."

Andrew's mouth fell open in sheer shock, and it wasn't until Dr. Craig stepped fully into the light from the skylights and extended a hand that he came to himself with a start. "I beg your pardon ... I am honored ... but how—I thought—that is—"

"I made the acquaintance of Lady Claire some time ago, and when I was released from hospital recently she had the goodness to call."

"Call." He did not release her hand. She could not be real—this genius, this icon of engineering. But no, there were her fingers in his. Gently, she pried them out of his grip.

"Indeed. In the course of our conversations, she let slip that you have a conundrum of the mechanical kind here, and was good enough to bring me by to see it."

"See it."

Dr. Craig seemed unaware that Andrew was sounding more and more like a parrot. Or an echo. He could not seem to get his brain working. "Yes. Is this the apparatus here?"

The scientist walked toward the chamber, unwinding her scarf as she went, and the prosaic gesture seemed to clear his fog. "I say, Dr. Craig, how is this possible? I mean, of course the state of your health is none of my business, and I'm delighted to see you—honored that you would, um, honor us, but ... ten years? And you walked out of there just recently?"

How was it possible he had not heard of it? The papers should have been screaming the news in headlines two inches high.

Standing next to the chamber, she smiled over her

shoulder. "Yes, ten years. I must say, the modern treatments are most efficacious. Now—" She indicated the control panel with its levers and alarm horns. "—I understand you are attempting to increase the carbon density of coal by means of pure current, for use on the railroads?"

He struggled with incredulity on one hand and necessity on the other. But his situation was so dire that necessity won.

"Yes. In theory, it should work. But in reality, the application of current simply disintegrates the coal, or burns it up. I've tried every possible method and nothing has produced results. My partner is already soliciting interest from the railroad men, but without a working prototype it will remain just that—interest. And no orders that would give us our start."

Dr. Craig nodded. "My young colleague and I put our heads together yesterday and may have a solution for you."

How on earth had Claire convinced the finest mind in three generations to apply itself to his little problem? Andrew hardly knew whether to laugh or fall at her feet babbling his thanks.

From the pocket of her coat Dr. Craig drew a folded piece of brown paper, and spread it on a nearby workbench. He recognized Claire's neat hand—and then his mind snapped to full attention as he realized what the lines and curves meant.

"I've been going down the garden path all this time," he breathed. "It's not electricks that will solve it at all."

"Our conclusion exactly," Claire said. "You must rebuild the chamber."

"Tigg." He glanced around wildly. "Where is Tigg?"

"'Ere, sir." Tigg popped up at his right hand.

"We must begin immediately," he said. "I'll draw up a list of supplies we'll need. We won't wait to order them—I'll visit the metalworks myself. In the meantime, I want you to disassemble the chamber."

"Shame to waste that brand-new glass cylinder, sir."

"Oh, we'll need that. It's the acceleration engines that have to go. We'll need to make room."

"Mr. Malvern."

"Once we have the switches and cells, then I'll—"

"Mr. Malvern!"

He realized Claire was standing on the other side of the bench, arms akimbo, that schoolmarmish look upon her face. The look that always made him smile. In the excitement, he had managed to forget his pain, and now it swamped him all over again. "Yes?"

"Dr. Craig was speaking to you."

"My apologies, ma'am." It was a relief to look at the scientist instead of Claire. "I'm afraid in my enthusiasm I forgot my manners."

"That is quite all right. Enthusiasm has carried many a scientist forward. I would offer you my help, but I'm afraid I cannot."

"You cannot?" Claire's eyebrows rose. "Aren't you going to assist us? This new chamber will be based on your device. There will be papers to be written, patent applications to file—"

"You have my permission to do all that. Since the

sketches are yours, and the construction of the chamber will be yours, the papers and patents should be yours as well."

"I don't understand." Claire's voice sounded almost plaintive. Disappointed. "The theory—the concept—those are yours alone. One look at this device and everyone will know where it came from."

"Let me clarify my situation. The same gentlemen who would be reading those papers and approving those patents are those with whom I dealt most recently." A look passed between them that Andrew couldn't read. "Do you imagine that they would receive them now without the same consequences as before?"

"Oh," Claire said faintly. Her face had gone pale.

Andrew began to feel a little uneasy. Something was amiss here.

"However, if you present the device and the chamber works as we believe it will, then regardless of what it *looks* like, my name need never come into the conversation. I will not sully the waters by becoming involved even at these early stages. I have set you on the path, and I know that your minds are equal to the task." She smiled at Claire with approval and—could it be true?—fondness. "I consider you the heiress of my past achievements. You are welcome to them. But it is time for me to move on to other fields."

"What fields?" Andrew couldn't help himself.

"Far-off fields. Those in the Canadas and the Americas, perhaps. I should like to see New York, and even Edmonton. I hear the diamond mines have made it nearly the equal of San Francisco for elegance and society."

Claire's mouth opened and closed, and finally words came out. "But your financial situation—I can assist to a certain degree, but a transatlantic airship ticket is no small matter."

"You have done quite enough to assist me," Dr. Craig said. "I am in your debt always, and if you should ever need anything, you have only to ask. But as to your kind concern, when things began to deteriorate all those years ago, I took the precaution of depositing a certain sum that my devices had brought me in a French bank. If I can get to Paris, I will have all the money I need."

"The packet leaves from the airfield at Hampstead Heath every day at noon," Andrew said, speaking automatically while his mind spun. Why should a scientist of her caliber flee the country? Why was she in Claire's debt if the latter had merely called upon her during her incarceration? Why should she not stay and reap the fame and benefits of her inventions? Times had changed. She was no longer the only woman in the Royal Society of Engineers—in fact, there were some among the younger generation who venerated her in the same way people venerated the Queen.

As for her time in Bedlam, well, it was quite clear that however she had gone in, when she came out she was perfectly sane. Such an ordeal could only add to her mystique.

"I'm afraid I don't understand either," he said at last. "Your career was brilliant. You could have all of Wit London at your feet. In fact, once the newspapers find out that you're free, I have no doubt you'll—"

Dr. Craig's hand came down on the drawings with the sound of a pistol shot. "The newspapers must not find out. The price of my help is your silence. No one must know I have been in London until I am well out of it. I must have your word."

"But—but why?"

"My reasons are known to Lady Claire and young Tigg here, and go no further. Your word, sir."

"You have it, of course," he said slowly. "I shall tell no one of your presence here, and we will present the new device as if it were our own. Though something in me balks at misrepresenting your work in that way."

"You may represent it however you like. Your discretion is all that matters to me." She turned to Claire. "I should like to return home now, please. I do not feel safe in a place where anyone might walk in."

"Of course. Mr. Malvern, I shall be back directly. Tigg, you stay here."

"Sure, Lady. I 'ave my work cut out for me anyways."

And so Andrew stood there as Claire and Dr. Craig wound their scarves about their hair, and watched them walk away—the greatest scientist London had seen in years, scurrying out of town like a thief, and with her the young woman he had not had the wits to court when he had the chance.

The door closed behind them and he turned to find Tigg already in apron and gloves, hard at work on the great brass cowling that held the glass chamber in place. "You aren't going to tell me what's going on, are you?"

HER OWN DEVICES

Tigg shook his head. "It ent worth the risk, sir. Would you like either of them two on your tail, mad as hornets and with ten times the sting?"

Andrew had to confess that he would not.

Claire slipped into the laboratory after having returned Dr. Craig to the cottage. She had left her in the hands of the Mopsies, who, upon hearing of her imminent departure, claimed her remaining time for the walking coop. Claire had no doubt that by the time she returned for dinner, the coop's leg mechanisms would have been constructed and would be lurching around the garden, followed by a squawking and deeply offended Rosie.

The sounds of clanging and tinkering told her that Tigg and Mr. Malvern were engrossed in adapting the chamber to its new purpose, so she climbed the stairs and seated herself at the desk with pen and paper.

Purchase airship ticket to Paris. (Safe to travel under own name?)
Visit bank for loan of traveling cash.
Underground to airfield or landau (recognition)?
Disguise? (Hair color? False padding?)
While at ticket office, inquire re self and 5 children to Cornwall.

A scrape of boot heels on the stairs brought her head up, and she smiled as Andrew emerged. He looked startled, and she hastened to reassure him. "I am not trying to usurp your place, I promise." She stuffed the paper into her reticule and capped his fountain pen. "I was merely making a list."

"You looked perfectly well behind the desk, and you know you may do as you like up here." He picked up a book teetering on a stack, then put it down again.

"Those are to go on the shelves, there, as soon as I find somewhere to put the stacks of treatises." But he did not seem concerned with her organizational abilities, though he had hired her for them. "Mr. Malvern, what is it? Are you disturbed by Dr. Craig's essentially giving away her devices to us?"

He gazed at her a little blankly. "What? Oh, yes. Yes, I am. Singular, I would say. I have so many questions, I hardly know where to begin." He seemed to come to a decision. "But I suppose the first one I must ask is, is it really true that you are engaged to be married to my partner, Lord James Selwyn?"

This was so far from what she'd expected him to ask that for a moment she couldn't think of the correct answer. "Oh, dear." James really was broadcasting it far and wide. All of a sudden her corset seemed very constricting, and she stood to try and get a breath.

"Oh, dear? My assistant engages herself to my partner without telling me about it, and all she has to say is 'oh, dear'?"

"James told you?"

"*James*, is it? Strange how I never thought you two were even on a first-name basis, much less making wedding plans."

"We have made no plans. The wedding is four years off at least."

"I should hope so," he muttered furiously to the bookcase. "He's robbing the cradle otherwise."

Is that how he saw her? As a helpless schoolgirl who couldn't be trusted to know anything about the world? "I shall be eighteen in two months. I'm hardly a child."

I am the Lady of Devices, and I broke Dr. Craig out of Bedlam two nights ago so that we could help you in your blasted experiments, and this is the thanks I get? To be berated and belittled by a scientist who wouldn't be able to complete his dissertation without me?

She ground her teeth together in an effort to keep her temper. "He very properly asked my mother for my hand, and proposed to me at his home last week. No robbing of any kind took place."

"Oh, no?" He gave a bitter laugh. "And why so extended an engagement? When two people are in love, they usually want to be bound for life immediately."

Why on earth did the news displease him so? Why was he being so unkind? "I told him I would be applying to enter The University of London in the fall, and would do my best to complete the four-year degree in three."

"You're engaged to a baron and you're going to *university*?" He dropped the folio he was pretending to leaf through, and it landed on the stove with a splat. Fortunately, no fire was lit.

"Of course. You knew that."

"But Claire, when a woman's future is assured, she hardly needs that kind of education."

"I don't understand you. Of course she does."

"So that on those occasions when you're not entertaining members of parliament and their wives, or drinking tea with Her Majesty, you can putter with your fleet of landaus out in the garage?"

This was interesting. "James has a landau?"

"No!" he practically shouted. "I'm speaking metaphorically, you aggravating creature. The point is, Lady Selwyn doesn't need a university education. She doesn't have to make her living like the rest of us, and it's a waste of time to pretend she does. Some other deserving person should have that seat."

"Metaphorically speaking," she said crisply, "Lady Selwyn will do as she likes. James has already agreed to it."

He gazed at her in utter perplexity. "What leverage did you use on him?"

"None at all. I merely stated what my goals were, which was to work for you so that you could provide a letter of reference for me, and to apply for the engineering program, beginning in the fall. I will need that letter by the end of the month, in case you are wondering."

"And if I don't give it to you?"

She leveled a long look at him. "Is my performance lacking in some way?"

"Of course not."

"And my collaboration with Dr. Craig, is that not going to be of use to you?"

"You know it is."

"Then why would you threaten me with such a thing?"

"Because—because, deuce take it—" He crossed the room in one stride, yanked her up against him, and—

Kissed her.

Desperately—deeply—

Ohhh.

Claire's knees went weak and she clutched at his lapels, her hands moving of their own volition while she fell into his kiss, spiraling into the delicious darkness, tasting him, opening to him, surrendering to him ...

This is what it's like.

This.

This is what I have been waiting for, and never knew.

He broke the kiss and she gasped for air, stumbling back to fetch up against the heavy desk. He turned away, breathing as though he had just run from one end of London to the other.

"I'm sorry, Claire. That should never have happened."

She could not speak. She was dazed with wonder and with her first taste of pleasure.

"It was a mistake, and I've dishonored both you and James. Please accept my apology."

A mistake? How could something so wonderful be a mistake?

Of course it was. She was engaged to James, whom she could not imagine kissing.

Committed to a man she did not love, and for what? To use him as a cloak? A social disguise so that she could carry on her nocturnal activities without reprisal?

For the first time, Claire realized the price that she

would be required to pay.

No. I will not pay it.

There must be some other way.

She would extricate herself from her engagement at once, and then she would be free to kiss Andrew again.

The Lady always found a way.

HER OWN DEVICES

13

The door closed downstairs. At first, Claire thought it might be Tigg, going out to the landau to fetch something, but no, there were feet on the stairs with a much heavier tread than his.

James Selwyn emerged, removing his gloves.

Andrew turned away, and Claire bent to the nearest stack of papers, tapping them into order with absolutely no idea of what they were.

James glanced between them, apparently seeing no hint of what had just transpired. "Good morning, Andrew. Ah, Claire. I was delighted to see the landau outside just now."

"I'm usually here in the mornings." Drat. That wasn't very welcoming. She was engaged to him. "I trust you are well?"

"Very well. You know, it occurred to me I have no idea of your address, so I cannot forward the invitations that have begun to arrive."

"Invitations?"

"I'm afraid I mentioned our happy news to one or two people—" Andrew exhaled sharply, but he didn't seem to notice. "—and now I am inundated by tubes. Tomorrow night, for instance, we are invited to the theatre with my cousin and his wife, and thence to Lady Wellesley's ball. On Friday there is dinner and cards with the Meriweather-Astor clan, and the next evening some kind of fancy-dress nonsense rumored to be attended by the Prince of Wales." He smiled at her. "My social life has doubled since I took myself off the marriage market. It's mystifying."

"It's not mystifying at all," Andrew said shortly. "Everyone knows Claire's circumstances. They simply want to be entertained by seeing the two of you together."

"Are you implying there is something amusing in my fiancée's situation?"

"It's no secret that she has to make her own way in the world. Those—those meringues are going to be at many of these events, and you've seen how they amuse themselves at her expense."

"I am standing right here," Claire reminded them both. "I'm not afraid of Julia and her set. I have more important things than *their* opinion with which to occupy my mind."

James smiled again, but it seemed a little tighter this time. "Then you will accompany me?"

HER OWN DEVICES

An idea popped into her head, fully formed, and she had difficulty controlling the urge to laugh. "You may accept on my behalf for the fancy-dress ball. As to the others, I'm afraid I have nothing suitable to wear. I left all my evening clothes behind at Carrick House, which was subsequently looted."

"I'm sure my cousins' wives can find you something."

"No, thank you, I could not put them to that trouble."

"Claire, you're going to have to meet my family eventually."

"Yes, I know, and in four years I am sure I will have many opportunities. But for this week, I simply have too much to do, and too little time in which to do it."

"Is Andrew working you that hard?" He glanced at him, censure in his gaze. "If that's the case, I'll have a thing or two to say about it."

"You shall not," Claire retorted. "I'm quite capable of managing my work here without interference."

"I'm entitled to interfere. You forget who is funding this endeavor—including your salary."

"I shall forego my salary, in that case."

This seemed to take him aback. "You don't mean it. What will you live on?"

"Until we are married, that is my business."

He gazed at her, perplexed. "Perhaps I was a little hasty," he said carefully. "Please forgive me." The tension in her shoulders did not relax, but she inclined her head. "I have another matter to discuss with you."

"If it is another ball, the subject is beginning to fatigue me." She swept the treatises from their shelf into one arm, and carried them across the room. Then she began to shelve books.

"No, not another ball, though you may as well resign yourself to them. They aren't going to go away. This is a more personal matter."

"Please excuse me," Andrew said. "I should not be an unwelcome third in this conversation."

"Relax, Andrew." Lord James waved his concern away. "I simply wanted to say that among the invitations was one from Claire's mother, Lady St. Ives."

She gripped a stack of books as if it would shield her from whatever he was going to say. "Did she want a wedding date for the announcement in the *Times*?"

"Yes, but I took care of that. She invited us down for a few days, that is all. I believe she wrote to you about it as well." When Claire nodded, he went on, "It just occurred to me that if I decline most of the other invitations, we could take the *Princess Mary* down and be back in time for the fancy-dress ball Saturday evening."

"Go by airship? Not the train?"

The *Princess Mary* was the air equivalent of the Flying Dutchman—though of course it traveled much, much faster. Going to see her mother in Lord James's company was the very last thing she wanted to do ... but at the same time, what better way to smuggle Dr. Craig out to the airfield and get her on the packet to Paris than as part of her own party?

"It will be dreadfully expensive."

"For two people? Hardly. I can send a tube and make the reservations at once."

"For seven."

"Seven?" He dropped his walking stick and had to bend to pick it up. "Are you planning to take my entire family?"

"No, mine. I should like the children to go, as well." She held up a hand and counted them off on her fingers. "Margaret, Elizabeth, Willie, Tigg, and Jake." As her lieutenant, Snouts would need to stay behind in her place. She would, unfortunately, need to leave the lightning rifle behind, and she could entrust its care to no one else. "I believe you've met everyone except Jake."

For a moment, all he could do was stare, and then he closed his mouth with a snap. "Certainly not."

"I shall buy their tickets myself, so they will not presume upon your generosity."

"I'm not going all the way to Cornwall with a passel of brats who don't even belong to me!"

"They are my responsibility, therefore, they go with me."

"Aren't you taking your governessing a little too seriously? Where are their parents?"

Time to take the plunge. "They have no parents. They are orphans. I have taken it upon myself to see to their education and well-being, and I think a journey to Cornwall will be beneficial to both."

"Why ... why didn't you tell me this?" James looked to Andrew for support. "Did you know?"

Poor Andrew looked as though he would rather be anywhere but in his own office. "I knew some of it. But it isn't really my business what Claire chooses to do with her private life. My business is the four hours she and Tigg spend here."

"Well, the rest of it is my business! I won't have it, Claire."

She gazed at him and for the space of two seconds there was silence in the room. Even downstairs in the laboratory, the sounds of banging and clanking had stopped. Then she lifted an eyebrow. "Until four years are up, my life is not your business. You surprise me, James. Would you begrudge a penniless orphan the chance to see an airship, to travel in civilized company, and to see a great estate like Gwynn Place?"

"It's not a matter of begrudging. The point is that they have nothing to do with me, and I don't care to be imposed upon."

"They are not imposing upon you in the least. They are my responsibility, and I propose it as an educational and social opportunity."

"Ridiculous."

She put the books on the shelf in a neat row. "As ridiculous as your balls and dinners. Very well. I decline all invitations, and you may explain to your circle in any way you like why your fiancée will not appear with you at any of your engagements."

For a moment he appeared to struggle with himself. "Claire, please."

Her voice quiet, she said, "It is the responsibility of the noble and blessed among us to look out for those who are less fortunate. The children will not bother you. I will not beg, but I will ask you to think of their well being—and my own."

Was he grinding his teeth? No, she was imagining it.

"I suppose you will do what you like, no matter what I say."

"Certainly. But my mind would be greatly eased if I knew I had your approval."

"I don't know if I can manage approval."

"I would be satisfied with unwilling complicity."

"It is safe to say you will have that."

Her smile seemed to make his face soften. At least, his jaw had stopped working. "Thank you, James. If you will be so good as to make the reservations for to-morrow's flight, I will pay for the children's tickets."

"Certainly not. In for a penny, in for a pound, I suppose."

She savored her victory. All in all, perhaps it would be best if she didn't mention the sixth member of their little party.

After all, he could hardly pitch a tantrum if the scientist were standing right in front of him, could he?

"Cor," Tigg breathed, gazing up with huge brown eyes at the enormous elliptical shape of the airship over his head, "I ent never seen anything so big in all me life. Not even bleedin' Parliament."

Even Jake, who rarely reacted to anything with more than a snort or clenched teeth, did not seem to be aware that his mouth had fallen open as he gazed up past the gleaming wood and brass gondola, to the mooring ropes that held the ship to the ground, to the polished canvas of the balloon itself as it swelled over their heads.

Jake had not wanted to come. "Ent never had my feet further off t'ground than t'Whitechapel catwalks, and never plan to," he said, and it had taken all the Mopsies' wheedling and all the other boys' teasing to get him to agree. It was Snouts who tipped the scale in the end. "The Lady needs protection, mate, and yer the best 'and I got," he'd told Jake in a low voice. "I don't trust his bleedin' nibs and nor should you."

Tigg, evidently, had blabbed the entire debacle up in the loft to a rapt audience. Claire was not certain she wanted her personal business common knowledge in the cottage, but it couldn't be helped. If it got Jake to go with them, she was willing to make the sacrifice.

"Any sign of his lordship, Mopsies?" she murmured. They never missed a thing, and getting Dr. Craig onto this airship with no one recognizing her was vital.

"Still in the bar, Lady," Lizzie said from her post on the walkway above. "He don't even know we're here yet. I 'ope 'e don't get sick."

Lizzie's only contact with boats, floating or flying, had been on the Thames, and nausea had been the result. Claire hoped that her stomach would stand up to the test today.

"Come, Dr. Craig. The steward appears to be beckoning to us."

"Tickets, ladies? We cast off lines in five minutes."

Dr. Craig handed him the ticket that had come in the tube this morning, and he stamped it and handed it back. "A pleasure to have you aboard, ma'am. Your seat is second from the bow. Please strap yourself in until we reach cruising altitude."

HER OWN DEVICES

Dr. Craig drew a shuddering breath through her nose, and her skin turned white as paper. "Doc— Rosemary?" Claire had agreed not to use her last name aloud. "Are you all right?"

The scientist controlled herself. "Must I be ... strapped in?"

Claire felt the cold brush of the woman's fear on her own skin. Of course. Leather straps.

"It's for your own safety, ma'am. The *Princess Louise*, she's eager to fly. If you're not prepared, you can lose your balance when we take off, what with the speed of ascent and all. But of course you can unbuckle them and move about the gondola as you please when the captain gives the all clear."

Slowly, she nodded. "Very well. It ... helps to know I can take them off myself." She turned to Claire. "I suppose this is where we bid each other farewell."

"I suppose it is." Claire gave her a warm smile. "I hope someday to see you again."

"I do, too." She turned to the others. "Margaret, remember ... the leg mechanisms must be oiled regularly, and you must exercise the coop at least once a week. Otherwise, you will find it unwilling to move when you really need it."

"Yes, ma'am." Maggie gazed up at her and took her hand. "Ta for your 'elp, ma'am. We would never 'ave figured out those legs without you."

"Yes, you would, little gumpus." The scientist's gaze softened. "I have every confidence in the inventiveness of your intellect. Goodbye, Master Tigg, Master Jake. I look forward to seeing all of you in the Canadas someday. I expect you will take them by storm." She knelt and took Willie in her arms. "And goodbye to you, darling. I shall never have children now, but if I had had any, I should have liked them to be like you."

The steward offered his hand and she mounted the steps, which since they did not actually rest upon the ground, dipped under her weight. As Claire moved everyone back, they could see her take her seat through the oval windows, and in the next moment someone shouted "Up ship!"

The lines were cast off, the mooring mast released the ring in the bow, and the *Princess Louise* leaped into the sky. In the space of a breath, she was the size of a gold piece next to the sun, and then she passed behind a cloud and was gone.

"That's a relief," Claire said. "I didn't think anyone would recognize her after all this time, but you never know."

"Recognize whom?"

She nearly jumped out of her shoes as James's voice boomed right behind them. She shot a poisonous glare at Lizzie, who had been watching the ship with her head tilted back and her hand shading her eyes, instead of keeping an eye on James's whereabouts.

"Oh, no one," she said easily. "I just thought I saw an old friend of Mama's, that's all."

"None of your gadding down here. It isn't safe. Come, they've just called for us to board."

The *Princess Mary*, being a domestic vessel that did not need to cross the sea, was much smaller than the *Princess Louise*, but she was no less beautiful. After they had presented their tickets, James handed Claire into the gondola and waited with barely concealed impatience for the children to board behind her. Jake stuck to her side as though he had been strapped there.

"Excuse me, you young ruffian, but I will sit beside my fiancée, thank you very much."

It wasn't until the steward explained that they could not all sit on one side ("The gondola will not trim, young sir. You must counterbalance the lady's weight by sitting in the corresponding seat on the port side.") that Jake grudgingly left her.

He did not relax his vigilance for the first hour, even during castoff, when he resolutely kept his gaze on Claire and not on the ground as they fell up into the sky. Tigg could barely keep his seat, straining against the leather harness as he pressed his nose to the window. "Lady, it's like a map down there, all laid out so tiny. Look, there's Windsor Castle!"

Claire had made this trip a number of times with her parents, but there was nothing more delightful than the awe of a child.

"Lady," Lizzie said faintly, "my stomach feels funny."

As James made a disgusted sound, Claire unharnessed herself and knelt by Lizzie's seat. "Come, dear. The ladies' lounge is to the rear of the gondola."

The steward appeared as if by magic. "Milady, you cannot move about yet. The captain has not given the all clear."

"You will have an unfortunate job of cleanup if my young charge does not reach the ladies' lounge in the next ten seconds, I fear."

His eyes widened. "Oh. Yes. In that case, let me escort the young lady."

Lizzie did not appreciate the novelty of a man offering his arm. Speed was of the essence, and they barely made it through the carved door and over to the gleaming metal sink in time. Lizzie rinsed her mouth and Claire gave her a peppermint. "When they serve lunch, I recommend eating lightly. Some soup and crackers, and perhaps a little fruit."

"But Lady." Lizzie's eyes filled with tears. "Those people behind us said there's to be chocolate macaroons! I ent never had such a thing."

"That, my dear, is what reticules are for. When we are on the ground again, the macaroons will be waiting for you."

Color began to return to Lizzie's pale face. "That ent stealin'?"

"Certainly not. Lord James paid your fare, and lunch is included. When you actually eat it is immaterial."

"I don't like 'is nibs, Lady."

"I hope you will not call him that to his face, Lizzie. His proper address is *his lordship*."

"I know it. He don't like us, so we don't like 'im."

"But if you were to give him reason to like you, then perhaps you might change your mind."

"He don't much like you, either, Lady. Leastways, not as we can tell."

This was a highly improper conversation to be having with a ten-year-old. But then, the Mopsies were not ordinary children. From what Claire had been able to discern, they had been living on the streets since they were knee-high. Self-preservation was a finely honed instinct, and the girls had not liked James Selwyn from the first.

"Lord James is used to the company of men, not ladies. He is brusque and wields authority, which we are not used to. He has asked me to marry him, though, so he must hold me in some esteem, wouldn't you say?"

Lizzie gazed at her while Claire adjusted her hair ribbon. "He don't show you respect, Lady. You gots to have respect to keep order."

Claire could hear the echo of Snouts's voice. "I have him in order, never you fear. Now, if you are feeling better, shall we return to the main salon before that poor steward is forced to come in after us?"

Lizzie clutched at the sleeve of her silk twill jacket. "Don't marry him, Lady. What will become of us?"

Ah. Here was the crux of the matter. It was a question that had teased Claire herself in the dark hours of the night. And now the answer came to her.

She knelt again, so that their eyes were on a level. "No matter what happens—whether I remain with you at the cottage, whether I marry James, or whether I take ship for South America to build bridges in the jungle—we will stick together for as long as we need to. We are flock mates, Lizzie. You, me, Maggie, Willie, the boys, Rosie ... all of us. Do you understand?"

It took a moment for her to nod. "Even if you marry 'is ni—his lordship and go to live in a castle?"

"I do not believe Selwyn Park is a castle, but yes.

Even if it were." Some might see such a promise as rash. But Claire saw beyond that to something greater. She and these children were in the process of becoming a family. If Lizzie—stubborn, willful, disobedient Lizzie—cared enough and was afraid enough to show what she really felt, then there was no way on earth Claire would promise or intend anything less.

To do so would make Claire herself less than she had been. The loss of this child's faith would mean a loss more terrible than she could repair.

A loss more terrible than that of James's regard.

"I'm—I'm feeling better now, Lady," Lizzie whispered.

"I am, too." She rose and took Lizzie's hand. "And I'm not talking about airsickness, either."

HER OWN DEVICES

14

"D'you mean your mum ent got a steam landau, Lady?" Tigg asked, aghast, when he caught sight of the carriage and four waiting for them outside the airfield at Truro. "And there's not a steambus in all of Cornwall?"

The shock of such provincialism kept him silent during the entire journey along the Carrick Roads, the great waterway that enabled seagoing ships to come and go between Falmouth and Truro. The north wing of Gwynn Place rose from the trees, and through the open carriage window they could hear the mewing of the gulls as they flashed and swung above the ocean.

When the carriage stopped under the portico, the great double doors opened and there stood Lady St.

Ives with Nicholas upon her hip. Claire dropped reticule and traveling case and covered her little brother with kisses, then gave her mother a more dignified hug.

"Mama, it is wonderful to see you."

"And you." Lady St. Ives ran a critical eye over her. "You've grown. Filled out. Changed, somehow, and yet it has only been a matter of weeks since I left you in town."

"More like two months, Mama. And here is James."

Her mother dimpled like a young girl and handed Nicholas to Claire so that she could envelop James in a hug. "I am so glad to welcome you to Gwynn Place. Do come in."

"Mama, I should like to introduce my young charges," Claire said firmly, the weight of her baby brother a comfort against her chest.

"Charges? I thought these were the tenants' children, being given a ride. What do you mean, charges?"

"I mean the young people for whom I am responsible. These young men are Jake, Tigg, and Willie. And the girls are Margaret and Elizabeth."

To Claire's astonishment, Lizzie and Maggie both dropped perfect curtsies, and Tigg bowed from the waist, as he had seen Andrew do that day in the Crystal Palace. Willie stood stock still, staring at Lady St. Ives as if seeing a vision.

Jake made a choking sound and turned away to haul Lord James's suitcase off the rack on top of the carriage before the coachman could swing it down to him.

"Do they not have—my goodness!" Lady St. Ives staggered back one step as Willie launched himself at her, hugging her legs through her voluminous skirts and bursting into tears. "Dear me, child, what on earth is the matter? Now, now. Dry those tears. Heavens, can you not—? Claire, what has possessed him?"

Try as she might, she could not detach the little boy from her mother's skirts. Even Jake stopped his busy work, his brows wrinkling in concern, as if he were half undecided as to whether Willie needed rescuing or not.

"Willie, darling ... it's all right." With the baby on one arm, Claire tried to put her other arm around the little boy. "You're quite safe. We're home now, at Gwynn Place, where I was born. You shall see Polgarth the poultryman, and the hens, and we shall picnic on the beach tomorrow and try not to have our toes pinched by crabs. Would you like that?"

Hiccupping, his face wet with tears, he gazed up at her mother. His mouth worked, but no sound came out. Claire had never seen anything quite so distressing. At last, Willie backed away and turned his face into Claire's collarbone as she knelt on the flagstones. His chest heaved with the effort not to cry—as if he were struggling with some disappointment too great to be borne.

"Ah, my little man," she whispered, the tears merely a breath away in her own throat. "What have you been through that you cannot speak of it?"

He merely clutched her tighter and did not answer.

"Dear me, such a perplexing group," Lady St. Ives said weakly, rescuing Nicholas and firmly affixing her best hostess smile. "I would ask why you feel responsible for them, but then we would be standing out here until dinner. Do come in. Lord James, Penhale will show you to your room. Claire, come with me and we shall sort out rooms for your ... charges."

Claire put on her best smile and led the little group up the grand staircase, along whose walls portraits of long-dead ancestors hung. There were more in the gallery, but these were of lesser importance. They merely welcomed guests; they did not impress them.

She had no doubt that she would be questioned within an inch of her life as soon as her mother got her alone. She'd been prepared for that. Having made the decision on the airship about the children's future went a long way to strengthening her resolution.

Along the gallery, then, through the sitting room and the morning room and the library, and up another staircase to the third floor. Male voices told her that James was being installed in the Blue Room, so called because of its bed hangings and its view of the sea. Her own room overlooked the rose garden, the orchard, and a piece of the poultry yard, just visible past a corner of the house.

"It's fairyland," Maggie breathed, turning to gaze from the yellow sprigged bed hangings to the sofa and chairs with their upholstery the color of a spring leaf. Gold trimmed the curlicues of her French Provincial dressing table and the matching mirrors on the wall, and the drapes were the same sprigged fabric as the bed, hanging the length of the double French doors that acted as windows. A balcony outside contained nothing but a bird feeder, broken and empty after a winter of disuse. She would have to fix that. "Does her ladyship sleep here?"

"Heavens, no," Lady St. Ives said from the doorway. "Our—my—room is the suite at the end, with a view of the sea. This is Claire's room."

"All this?" Maggie encompassed the space with both arms. "All for one person?"

Claire swung open a cabinet filled with books and papers, pencils, ink, and compasses. Good. Nothing had been removed. "Yes. I grew up here, remember." She moved to the bookshelves that flanked the bed, both containing the books that had been the companions of her lonely childhood. "See? We can read these stories at night. They're the ones I loved growing up."

A broad figure appeared behind her mother and Claire smiled. "Hello, Mrs. Penhale."

"Good evening, Lady Claire. I am happy to see you looking so well. Polgarth bids me tell you that Seraphina hatched sixteen chicks day before yesterday, and he hopes you will come to see them."

Lady St. Ives firmed her lips. "Not now, Claire. Mrs. Penhale, if you would be so good as to take these children upstairs and find beds for them?"

"Upstairs?" Claire left Maggie and Lizzie leaning over the balcony and crossed the room. Upstairs was where the servants slept, and no one would thank her for making them share their beds. "They are my guests, Mama. The girls can sleep here with me, and the three boys will all fit in the Raja's Room with acres to spare."

"Certainly not." Her mother eyed Jake, who had ranged to the end of the corridor and was gazing out at the sea as though he'd never seen it before. Perhaps he had not. "When was the last time that young man had a bath?"

"Last night, as it happens," Claire said tightly. "These children are our guests as much as Lord James is. I will not have them sent upstairs as though they were bootblacks and scullery maids."

"That young man could pass for a bootblack." Her mother lowered her voice. "And is the shorter one a *blackamoor*?"

"What?"

"The one you call Tigg—such an extraordinary name. The one whose skin is the color of coffee."

Claire stared at her in utter perplexity. "Tigg has the mind of an engineer and the quickest at that. What on earth has the color of his skin to do with anything?"

"Calm down, dear. I was merely remarking upon it."

"You would do better to remark upon something sensible, then, such as how well he maintains the steam landau. He can take it apart and put it together again as quickly as I can." Too late, her mother's eyebrows began to rise, and Claire realized what she had said. Well, there was nothing for it now. "Gorse taught me."

"Then I am devoutly thankful it did not come with you. Honestly, after visiting these children upon us, nothing you do will surprise me anymore. Fine, then. The girls will stay with you, if you insist. But upstairs the boys will go, and that is that. The second footman has engaged himself to that redheaded cook of Sir Richard's, so he has left an empty room. They can use that."

"Mother—"

By this time, Tigg and Jake had heard the fuss and hovered in the hall outside. "It's all right, Lady," Tigg said. "We c'n sleep on a pallet in the stable, if it comes to that. We done worse."

"Certainly not. You are my guests."

"If it's all the same to you, Lady, I wouldn't catch a wink in a room like this." Jake gazed at her dear sprigged curtains as though they might billow out and wrap themselves around his neck. "Upstairs might be less'n you want, but it's better'n we've 'ad lots of places."

"A sensible young man," Lady St. Ives said. "I don't know where you found that coat, but if you do not want to be mistaken for a bootblack, you must find another. You're about the size of my late husband's younger brother, who was lost at sea. Let me see if I can locate something of his for you."

Jake looked as though he wasn't sure about wearing the clothes of a dead man, but he had the sense not to argue. "Thank you, milady."

Another revelation. Claire had never before heard him thank anyone, either.

Since they were to dine *en famille* in the conservatory, there was no need for evening clothes. All the same, Claire looked through the dresses in her closet since tomorrow they were to go to Sir Richard's and she had nothing suitable. Everything looked impossibly young, not to mention short in the hems. She had grown since she was down last summer—grown and changed in mind as well as body.

The fact that she could carry a point with her mother and actually win was proof of that.

After the fresh-caught fish, salad, and ham, the hour grew late. A tour of the house and grounds was enough to exhaust Willie, and the girls began to fade as well. Claire put them to bed, said good night to Tigg and Jake, and girded her mind to return to the music room, where Lady St. Ives was entertaining James at the piano.

"Ah." Her mother ceased her cheery runs up and down the keys, and settled herself on the sofa. She patted the cushion next to her. "Come here, dear. We have much to discuss, and if I know you, you will go to visit Polgarth in the morning and that will be the last I see of you."

James leaned on the mantel, a thin cigarillo between his fingers. Rather pointedly, Claire crossed the room and opened the window, then seated herself and prepared to face the music.

"Dear James tells me that you are planning to go to The University of London in the fall, and your engagement will be a long one. Claire, you astonish me."

She ignored the last bit. "James is quite correct. That is why the announcement went in the *Times* without a wedding date."

"But why?" Her mother's eyes were genuinely distressed. "I cannot understand why you would not marry within six months, especially when you are living from hand to mouth—where are you living, exactly, if it is not with your great-aunts Beaton?"

"I have a cottage on the river, Mama, that is quite comfortable and meets the children's needs. I school them in chemistry and physics, arithmetic and reading, as well as outdoor pursuits such as climbing, walking, running, and gardening. We even have a chicken."

"And how did you come upon this ... cottage?" James inquired, turning the cigarillo in his fingers as if its incendiary properties interested him.

"I bought it," she said bluntly. "My income is quite up to the task, I assure you."

"You bought a cottage?" Lady St. Ives, who as an heiress had never done such a thing in her life, stared at her incredulously. "What income?"

"Really, mother, do you expect me to discuss such things in front of a gentleman?"

"Since your income is partly financed by me, I find the subject very interesting," James said. "I certainly don't pay you enough to buy cottages."

She lifted her chin. "Be thankful I don't ask you for a pay rise, then."

"Claire! I find this most distasteful. One does not accept pay from one's fiancé, much less joke about it. It's just not done."

"In your world, Mama, of course it isn't. But in mine, I see no reason why I should not be paid for the work I do. Joke though it is."

"You would not have to work at all if you would be sensible and marry James at Christmas like a normal person. I hope you do not expect me to finance this university nonsense. We are barely getting by here, and

Lord James is—" She glanced at him and stopped.

"Of course not. I do not expect James to finance it, either. I expect I will have to sell some of my shares in the Midland Railroad."

James fumbled his cigarillo, dropped it on the hearth, and was forced to toe it half smoked into the grate. But before he could say a word, Lady St. Ives waved Claire off, looking faint. "I cannot listen to you. Have the goodness to keep your commercial transactions to yourself. This topic is in the very worst of taste."

"I did say so earlier, Mama. Tell me, if we are to dine with Sir Richard tomorrow, might I borrow an evening dress? Every frock I owned was looted the night I left Carrick House."

"I suppose you will have grown out of your country clothes. Yes, I will see what Silvie can find for you. And while we are there, please have the goodness to keep these subjects to yourself. I am sure Sir Richard does not want to know."

"I can promise you that."

"I suppose there is no use attempting to persuade you to come and live here?"

"None at all, Mama. I am very happy where I am. I am doing satisfying work, and then there are the children."

"Ah yes," her mother said. "The children. Do you expect them to accompany us to dinner?"

"Of course not. Would you bring Nicholas?"

"No. Well, I must say, that is a relief. Mrs. Penhale will look after them in the kitchen."

"I'm sure they would much prefer that in any case. Tonight's dinner was enough of a trial. I'm afraid I haven't had much time for the finer points of their educations. Managing the basics keeps my hands full."

"Where exactly did they come from, if they do not even know a soup spoon from a dessert fork?"

"An excellent question," James put in.

A sound came from the hall outside. Probably the footman, lighting the electricks.

The silverware had been a trial, but Claire had done her best to show the Mopsies what each gleaming utensil was for. With the boys she had not been so successful, and they'd eaten their entire dinner with knife and spoon. "In the course of my getting settled, I met them and realized they would benefit from a mutual arrangement. We had much to teach each other. When the cottage came available, it seemed natural to include them so that their educations might continue."

"Yes, but who do they belong to?" her mother insisted. "Where are their families?"

"They are orphans."

"Did you adopt them from an orphanage? I simply do not understand how you can go from graduating from St. Cecelia's on one day to acting as a mother hen on the next."

"The riots changed everything, Mama."

"I am well aware of that, since I cannot sell that house for love nor money."

"Lady Flora, if I might suggest something?" James put in.

"Do, please. I so long for a man's guidance in these

matters."

Oh, good heavens. Surely she hadn't just fluttered her eyelashes at him? Claire frowned.

"The Wilton Crescent address is a good one, and the house is sound," James said. "It just needs repair and cleaning out. If you will sell it to me, I could offer you a good price for it." He turned his gaze on Claire. "And then Claire could move back in and live there in comfort while she pursues her education. When we are married, I will sell my town house and live there as well."

Another sound, like the scuff of a boot on carpet. No one seemed to notice but she. Perhaps her senses were more attuned to such things since she had to depend on them more.

Lady St. Ives clasped her hands in delight. "Oh, would you? His lordship bought that house when we were married, and it broke my heart to hear of it being mistreated by those vandals. It's a wonderful plan, James. Thank you from the bottom of my heart."

"What do you think, Claire?" James strolled to the sofa opposite and stretched his legs out in front of him. "Would you like to return to familiar ground?"

The invisible ropes of his will tightened around her shoulders and feet—she could almost feel their physical touch. Why had he never mentioned a word of this to her? On the outside, it seemed highly reasonable—generous—thoughtful. But on the inside ... there was the soft touch of the rope.

"I must confess, I've thought of it often," she said slowly. "There would certainly be enough room for the children, and—"

"I was not thinking of the children, Claire," he said. "I was thinking of you, going to classes, growing in intellect and confidence, and becoming the woman who will be my bride."

"That is kind and generous of you, James. But I must think of the children, since no one else can. They are my responsibility."

"Can you see that ragamuffin lot in Wilton Crescent?" Lady St. Ives leaned over and lowered her voice, though there was no one in the room but the three of them. "They would be arrested the moment they stepped into the garden."

"You must return them to where you found them and get on with your life," James said. "You must be reasonable. Think of it from my point of view. I want a family of my own, not five castoffs from who knows where running wild about the place."

Claire got up and closed the window. She was feeling chilled.

When she returned to her seat, she took the long way around the sofa, allowing her to see out into the hall. Aha. As she had suspected, Jake had not relaxed his vigilance. Snouts had told him to keep an eye on her, and he was fulfilling his duty to the letter. A movement behind him told her Tigg was with him.

She should feel perturbed that they had overheard the details of her finances—that they were witness to this loving grilling. But she was not.

In point of fact, it only made her more sure that she was doing the right thing. *You must. You must.* The last man who had said *You must* to her was no doubt still nursing his burns and mourning the loss of his future progeny.

"And what of my commitment, James? I gave the children my word that we would not be separated, no matter our circumstances."

"I suppose we should consider, then, which is more important—your commitment to a group of alley mice, or your commitment to me."

"They are not alley mice."

"Not any more, perhaps. Do not mistake me, dear. I admire your attempts to civilize them, spoons and forks notwithstanding. But you must look at the longer view."

If he said those two words to her once more ... Her trigger finger twitched, and she clasped her hands in her lap.

"So then, as I understand it, I may live in Carrick House until we are married, but I can only do so if I am alone."

"If you truly own this cottage, as you say, then the children can stay there, as long as there is some responsible person with them, of course."

"Otherwise they might return to being alley mice."

James inclined his head in agreement, completely missing the edge to her tone.

Very well, then. "Since I am educating them, such a scheme would not be practical. I prefer to live in my own home, thank you. But do not let this dissuade you from buying Carrick House, James. You must, of course, do as you like."

He looked so flummoxed she realized that he had not thought she might turn him down.

"Claire, I won't have it." Lady St. Ives leaped into the conversation once more. "You are not only ridiculous, you are unladylike to insist upon living with these children when a good man is perfectly willing to provide for you. I insist that you accept his offer and do as he suggests."

"I am very sorry, Mama, but I cannot. I will not go back on my word. If the children cannot live with me at Carrick House—and I mean all of them, because there are at least a dozen back at the cottage—then I cannot live there, either."

"There are more?" James's face was slack with disbelief. "How many indigent orphans have you been concealing?"

"I haven't been concealing any. You simply made an incorrect assumption about the five I have with me."

James rose abruptly and stalked to the window. "I give up," she thought she heard him mutter, but she couldn't be sure.

Lady St. Ives gazed at her. "I have brought you up and lived in the same house with you for seventeen years ... but I do not know you at all."

"I have grown up, Mama," Claire said gently. "I hope you will become acquainted with me as I am, not as you once wished me to be."

"Acquainted?" Her mother shook her head and rose gracefully from the sofa. "A good choice of words. One I never thought I would use of my own daughter."

And she swept from the room, never even noticing the two shadows that withdrew into the darkness as she passed.

15

It took a good hour with Polgarth the poultryman before Claire got her equilibrium back. Then, her delight in showing Maggie and Willie Seraphina's baby chicks washed over the memory of the previous evening, smoothing out the edges and softening the view.

Her mother loved her. James held her in some esteem. They were both concerned for her wellbeing, and it was not their fault that their way of expressing it was not only suffocating, but irritating to boot.

She knelt by the broody-house and pushed her thoughts away. She would not allow them to spoil her pleasure in the present.

Maggie was gazing up at Polgarth as though he held the keys to the kingdom. He smiled at her as he spoke.

"Seraphina is a Buff Orpington, of a purebred stock we developed right here at Gwynn Place. She's a good mum, she is. You see how she uses a special cluck to call to the chicks." The golden balls of fluff tumbled and ran to her, tucking themselves under her wings and in her breast feathers as the humans crowded around the little wood-and-wire house. "They've been listening to it in the egg, see, and that's how they know she's their mother." Willie tugged on the man's jacket, his brow furrowed in disbelief. "Oh, aye, young sir," Polgarth said, as if the boy had spoken aloud. "They can hear in the egg once they've developed enough. Now, there, Seraphina has realized that you mean her no harm, so the little 'uns are coming out now to see who's come to visit. Would you like to hold one?"

Willie nodded vigorously, and when the chick was deposited in his cupped hands, he touched it with gentle fingers. Maggie waited impatiently for a chick, and giggled with delight as it ran up her arm and nestled under her curls.

"Ah, ye have the gift, maid," Polgarth said. "Much as her young ladyship does."

"The gift?" Maggie tried to turn her head to see the little peeper by her ear.

"Aye. There's some as have it, and some as don't. If ye don't, ye can't see these hens as owt but meat. But we as have it, we see something different. We see the feathery people that they are, and they recognize it, they do. This little 'un has no fear of you."

Seraphina watched them with a suspicious eye, and Willie gave Maggie a nudge. "I see 'er. She thinks I might hurt the little 'un, but I won't."

Claire suppressed a smile as Maggie unconsciously echoed Polgarth's turn of phrase. "We have a hen at home, Polgarth, called Rosie. She is of uncertain parentage, but she rules the garden absolutely."

"Lewis is terrible afraid of 'er," Maggie told him. "But me and Lizzie, we saved 'er life in t'market and she knows it. We built 'er a walking coop, with steam-powered legs, see, so's we can take 'er with us when we leave."

"Did ye now? I should like to see such a thing. But you know, this hen alone, that's not good. Chickens are flock birds. She must have companions."

Willie nodded and looked anxious. The chick was attempting to struggle out of his hands, and Polgarth took it gently.

"We're going to find companions for 'er," Maggie confided. Her chick had fluttered up on top of her head, where it stood like Christopher Columbus looking out at the New World. "But t'Lady has said we're not to steal any. They must be in need of rescue."

"Her ladyship is right," Polgarth said solemnly. "Stealing is not for the likes of you. But rescue, now, that is a noble task." He held out a hand, and the chick ran onto it. He restored it to Seraphina, who relaxed visibly when all her brood were around her again.

"Maggie! Lady!" Lizzie came panting around the corner from the rose garden. "Jake says Cook 'as made us a basket and it's time to go to the shore."

"I don't want to go to the shore," Maggie said. "I want to stay here with Polgarth."

Lizzie's eyes widened and Claire wondered if this was the first time they had ever been of two minds about something. "But you must come. We ent never seen the shore."

"I'll see it tomorrow."

"But Mags—"

"You 'eard what Jake said about what 'is nibs thinks of us. I ent goin' if he's goin'. Chickens is much nicer."

"What did Jake say?" Claire asked softly, the edge back in her tone.

"That Lord James don't want us to live wi' you. 'E called us a bunch of alley mice." She turned a pleading gaze on Claire. "You ent goin' to do what he says, are you?"

"Certainly not. I made you a promise and I shall keep it."

"What if he don't want to marry you, then?" Lizzie wanted to know.

"Then I shall bear that sorrow as best I can."

Not one of her companions, with the possible exception of James, had ever seen the sea.

The sand, a pale gold color unique to Cornwall, stretched in a narrow ribbon along the cliffs above the Carrick Roads. With the wind tugging at her hair, Claire tucked up her skirts into her waistband and hung her shoes around her neck. Navigating these cliffs required bare feet, and the reward would be the soft sand.

In seconds, Lizzie had followed suit. Maggie had remained with Polgarth, but Claire had no doubt her sister would chivvy her down here tomorrow.

The path down to the sand was more overgrown than it had been when she lived here, but that did not stop her nimble descent. She, Lizzie, and the boys had run to the water's edge and let the waves cream over their toes before James and his elegant kid boots even reached the bottom.

"Lady, you were mad to leave this place," Lizzie sighed. "It really is bleedin' fairyland."

"How much belongs to you?" Jake asked. He gazed at his feet as the waves sucked the sand from under them and a tiny crab came to investigate.

"As far as you can see." Claire waved a hand to the south. "And to the ferry on the north."

"Cor," Tigg breathed. "If you only 'ad proper steam vehicles down 'ere I'd never leave."

"Steam vehicles, and a university, and manufactories from which to obtain parts for inventions," Claire added. "London has its faults, but you must admit it is a good place for putting one's intellect to work."

"But Gwynn Place is for putting one's knowledge of the land to work," said Lord James, coming up behind them. "And for restoring the spirit by growing close to nature again."

He had not removed his shoes, and placed his feet carefully.

"You may explore as far as you like," Claire said to the children. "There are caves about a half mile that way, once used by pirates to smuggle in brandy from

France. I used to find silver pieces in there, and—"

With a whoop, they were off and running.

"We shall have lunch in an hour," Claire called after them. When she turned, James had unfolded a blanket on the warm sand and managed to sit on it without bringing even a grain of sand with him.

She was not so careful. But the sun felt wonderful on her bare feet and on her face.

"You should have brought a hat," James observed. "You will be tanned ... more."

"The gulls don't care, and neither do the children."

"Ah, yes. The children."

"James, if you plan to lecture me again, you may save your breath to cool your tea."

"Now you're beginning to sound like them."

"I am simply stating a fact. And here is another. I am very sorry you and I do not agree about the depth of my commitment to them. I mean that, truly."

His gaze softened under the brim of his bowler hat. "I am glad to hear it. You had me worried."

"Do not mistake me. I shall not change my mind. But I do wish we could have found some common ground."

Why was she even drawing out this charade? She had known going in that she did not intend to marry him, so why continue the deception? She must simply break their engagement here and now, while they had both time and privacy.

When she did, her heart and mind would be free to think about kissing Andrew Malvern. There would be no more guilt, no more shame. At the very least, she had things in common with him. What did she share with James, really, except a common upbringing and an interest in locomotives?

She must have been mad to accept his offhand proposal, and the worst sort of flirt to behave as his fiancée when she did not intend to be his wife. There was the protection of his name if her underground activities caught up with her, but even that did not seem worth the price.

And what of his regard for her? She had no idea if it even existed. But even if it did not, she had wronged him the moment she had allowed Andrew to kiss her.

Oh yes, she could serve up a heaping plate of shame without half trying. She was better than this. Best to have it out now.

"James?"

"Yes, dear?"

"Do you love me?"

She could feel him turn to gaze at her, but she faced into the breeze, looking out to sea. "And what has brought this question on now, instead of on the day I proposed?"

"I have had time to think, and to weigh options, and to look into the future."

"It sounded to me as though you had the future planned out, and I was to stand aside and allow you to put the plan into action."

Goodness. How soft his tone was, and how cutting. "I do have plans."

"Yes, but on close observation, I cannot see that they include me."

She was silent, allowing the truth to speak for itself. Then she said, "Shall we call it off, then?"

"I will of course abide by your wishes, but I must tell you that your mother and I have already come to an agreement. You do not have much in the way of a dowry, but Carrick House is to be signed over to me in lieu of that sum."

"I thought you were going to buy it?"

"No. Your lady mother and I had a little talk last night in her private parlor. She is most anxious to see you settled."

So anxious that she would sign over Claire's lovely house to a stranger. Oh, she would be living there, true enough. But it would never be hers, in her own right, as it would have been before the riots according to the terms of her father's will. As the cottage was hers now.

"In fact, she was most insistent that I not allow you to attend university. A wedding by Christmas was the price of the house, in fact."

The ropes. Sliding, whispering, snaking around her. Invisible and potent, they would tie her down as a spider tied down a fly until it was convenient to eat it.

"It would be difficult to agree to such a plan if I were not willing," she said, her mouth dry.

"You are not yet eighteen, and therefore under her authority."

"I am under no one's authority but my own, James. Let us be clear on that."

"A Wit point of view, to be sure, but one that is not upheld by the law."

"I shall be eighteen in October. Her authority will

have ended before Christmas."

"You will note that I said *by* Christmas. I understand it is lovely in Cornwall at Yuletide, particularly for a delayed honeymoon."

"Delayed?"

"Yes. October is an unseasonable time to travel, what with the shooting and hunting parties. Much better to save family visits for the winter, when one expects and indeed looks forward to indoor pursuits."

Now she did look at him, swinging around so she could see his eyes while these outrageous things came out of his mouth.

"Are you saying my mother has agreed that we should be married when I turn eighteen, with complete disregard for my plans and hopes and promises to others?"

"In essence, yes."

"I shall not."

"I am very much afraid that you must. Come, Claire. You have already agreed to be my wife. Why is that so distasteful to you now, when it does not seem to be four years hence?"

"You know why. Lady Selwyn cannot, of course, attend university." Well, perhaps she could, but not without enormous effort at lifting the heavy, suffocating strictures of society. The Lady of Devices could attend classes and invent and laugh and breathe the free air just as she pleased, with no one the wiser and no one to tell her she could not.

She was not Lady Selwyn. Not yet.

"Nor can she act as governess to impecunious children," James went on. "Or live unchaperoned in a house heaven knows where."

He would take from her everything she valued. And for what? What would this accomplish except the acquisition of a wife who hated and resented him?

"Why are you doing this, James? If you know I wish to be free to pursue my degree on my own terms, why are you risking the utter loss of my regard by forcing the issue?"

Now it was his turn to look out to sea, as if the answer could be found in the spindrift on the waves. Following his gaze, she saw figures in the distance. The children were on their way back from the pirates' caves.

"I want a family, Claire," he said simply.

The roaring dragon of her rage sat down abruptly, and coughed on its own flame.

"I want a woman who is brave and principled and intelligent, so that the best qualities of us both can be passed to our children. I want someone who is not a meringue, who will stand by me and face the adventures of life without flinching. Someone who will raise children who can make their way in a new world that may not run on Blood principles. I have had this list in my mind for years, and until I met you, it was just a list. But now it has flesh and form. It has become a real woman. You."

"James, I—"

"I know you don't love me yet. I know you don't like my high-handed ways. But Claire, along with being a Selwyn, I'm also a man of parts. And one of those parts drives a hard business bargain. If I'm too forceful, it's only because I don't want to lose what I've found."

The dragon hung its head, quenched and frowning, tortured by the memory of another man's kiss.

And then the children were upon them, shouting something about pirate silver, and the opportunity to answer him for good or ill was lost.

HER OWN DEVICES

16

Much to Claire's relief, when it came time to say good-bye and climb into the carriage for the trip back to the Truro airfield, Lady St. Ives did not bring up the subject of their engagement. Claire was sure that she had hashed it out with Lord James in yet another private *tête-à-tête*, and trusted him to carry the day.

Instead, her mother gazed at Willie as Claire helped him mount the steps of the carriage. "Strange," she murmured. "That child looks so familiar, and I simply cannot place him at all. It has been bothering me since you arrived, and I am no closer to an answer than I was on Tuesday."

"Truly?" James was already inside, along with the rest of the children, and Claire stood alone beneath the portico, waiting for a final hug goodbye. "I am quite certain you have never met before this."

"As am I," her mother replied. "But the widow's peak, the eyes ... depend upon it, I will wake in the middle of the night with the answer, and by that time you will be back in London."

"Then you must send me a tube." Claire leaned in and hugged her, breathing in the scent of lilies. "You must also tell me what develops with Sir Richard," she whispered. "I saw how he looked at you at dinner the other night."

"Oh, pshaw." Lady St. Ives flushed and shook out the black crystal-pleated chiffon at her wrists. "I am in mourning and it is not appropriate to say such things. Goodbye, dear. I wish you a safe journey."

During the flight back, it was almost comical to see how the Mopsies' attitude toward such a mode of travel had changed. This time, they were the experienced ones—quite possibly experts in the field, if the way they bossed some businessman's little sons about the gondola was any indication. And Lizzie's stomach appeared to be equal to the challenge—and the macaroons.

When they landed at Hampstead Heath and the airship had been moored to its mast once again, Lord James escorted them to the Underground station. "Are you sure I cannot give you a ride in the carriage, Claire? It is hardly suitable for my fiancée to be running about on trains."

"I invest in them and so do you. There is nothing wrong with trains." It was the fact that working people used the Underground that bothered him, not the method of transportation itself. Hmph.

"You just don't want me to know where you live. This cottage on the river is either a dream or a disgrace."

"It all depends on your point of view," she retorted with airy ease. "So, then, a fancy-dress ball at Wellesley House tomorrow evening? Shall I meet you there?"

Surely by then she could think of a way to extricate herself from an emotional tangle that was becoming deeper by the day.

"Certainly not. You must allow my carriage to fetch you so that we may arrive together, the way an engaged couple might actually do."

"So that you may grill your coachman as to my address? No."

"Claire, you're being unreasonable. This secrecy is not only inconvenient, it is ridiculous."

She reined in her temper. "I am never unreasonable. Your coach may fetch me at the laboratory at eight, which is neither inconvenient nor ridiculous. Listen—I can hear the train. Into the tunnel, girls, or we shall miss it. Thank you for a lovely trip, James," she called over her shoulder as, bags in hand, they ran helter-skelter down the tunnel to the platform.

It was a relief to see the cottage as they walked across the Regent Bridge, and a greater relief to know that the chemists had not burned it down, nor had it been attacked by some South Bank rival in her absence.

There were, however, a number of chickens in the garden that had not been there before. "Snouts, where did these come from? What a motley lot. And how thin."

Before he spoke, he made a show of handing the

lightning rifle back to her, as if formally relinquishing command. "Me and some o' the boys were minding our own business up on the watch platform—"

"Snouts ..."

"Honest, Lady. It weren't our fault some bilge rat decided to take potshots at us from the river—I suspect our friend the Cudgel 'as called in a few chips—and when I returned fire, 'is barge began to take on water."

"But the chickens, Snouts?"

"They was on the deck, Lady, in cages," Lewis put in. "We barely got 'em off in the skiff afore the old wreck sank."

"You sank a barge and stole its cargo?" she said, aghast. "After I gave strict instructions that any birds were to be rescues only?"

"Lady, if that weren't a rescue, I dunno what you'd call it," Lewis protested. "Them bilge rats was swimmin' for the Chelsea Embankment fast as they could go, never mind that them cages was shut fast and them birds trapped in 'em."

"Poor birds was cover, like as not," Snouts said. "Stolen to make 'em look like an 'armless barge goin' t'Leadenhall from upriver."

Claire took a calming breath. That did make sense. "Then you did well, and I am happy that Rosie has at least a dozen minions to manage."

Even as they watched, a big black rooster flinched at Rosie's flashing beak, and bowed himself to the ground as she passed. The walking coop stumped up and down along the wall, scattering those few birds who had not already learned to keep out of its way.

"I see the coop is operating."

"Aye. Mopsies sent a tube with instructions," Lewis told her. "Doc said it was to be oiled an' exercised once a week, or it'd seize up."

"Excellent. You all deserve a reward for your heroic behavior. I shall see Granny Protheroe about the prospect of roast beef and Yorkshire pudding for dinner tomorrow."

The boys grinned and left her to herself.

Home. It might be humble, but how peaceful it was.

She settled on a kitchen chair and watched the Mopsies and Willie catch up to the coop, direct it over to the porch, and cool it down for the night. They removed the ladder from the watch platform overlooking the river—much to the dismay of the boy on watch, who would have to crawl through an upstairs window to go to bed—and leaned it against the door of the coop. As dusk fell, one by one the chickens gathered around the porch, where they could see Rosie in majestic repose up in the rafters. The girls gently persuaded them with handfuls of corn that the coop was the better option, until every one had mounted the six feet of ladder and was safe inside.

"What about Rosie?" Claire inquired. "She must become used to the coop as well."

"Can you reach her down for us?"

Once up on the chair, Claire could just slip a hand under the bird's feet. "Come along, your ladyship," she said, climbing down with her. "It's time for you to see your new quarters."

Rosie went, but only under protest. Soon, though,

the fuss behind the closed doors settled down, and Claire waved the girls inside much as they had just done with the birds, while Willie climbed into her lap.

Lizzie stopped at the door. "I liked that airship, Lady, and your house, and Polgarth and the chickens." Willie nodded vigorously in agreement. "But I like it 'ere, too."

"So do I, me dearie," she said in her best imitation of Polgarth's West Country drawl.

"So we won't be leavin', then, to go live in Belgravia?"

"No," she said in her own voice. "I am sorry to say that there is no room in Wilton Crescent for a dozen of us and as many chickens. We are forced to stay where we are."

Lizzie nodded, satisfied, and went in.

Willie touched the locket on her chest—one she'd had since childhood but had left in her treasure box at Gwynn Place. Lady St. Ives had put a daguerreotype of Nicholas inside it and pressed it into her hand when they'd said good night the evening before.

She opened it for him. "See? A picture of Nicholas, so I don't forget him."

Inexplicably, Willie's eyes filled with tears, and it was some time before she could calm his sobbing enough that they could go in to dinner.

"Lady, you'll be caught!"

Jake and Lewis gaped as Tigg handed her into the

steam landau. She pulled the lightning rifle out of its holster and tucked it under the seat, otherwise it would dig into her back as she drove. The buckles and clips of her corselet held their usual accoutrements, and her skirts were rucked up to her knees by their leather straps. A riding hat completed the raiding rig, with a black chiffon scarf tied round it in case she needed it, and her driving goggles perched on the brim.

"I think not, Jake."

"I thought you said you was goin' to a ball wiv 'is nibs, not on a firelamp run."

"I am. A fancy-dress ball." She indicated a Venetian leather mask hanging from a clip, bought that morning in Portobello Road. "The best disguise is to go in plain sight. I can't think of an ensemble more likely to accomplish that end, can you?"

"Make someone recognize you, more like."

"It's hardly likely anyone from the South Bank gangs will be at Lady Wellesley's ball. And if they are, it's for thieving, which I would be well equipped to prevent, don't you agree?"

"If you say so, Lady." Doubt laced his tone. "One of us orta go wiv you."

"Tigg will go with me as far as the laboratory, where he will wait with the landau, and his lordship is going the rest of the way." Jake made a sound that conveyed his opinion of his lordship's usefulness in a tight spot. "I will be all right, Jake. I'll have the rifle in its holster and a vial of gaseous capsaicin at my belt. Which I will not need, of course. These are civilized people, more interested in waltzing and gossip than in wrangling and stolen goods."

With that, she ignited the landau and pushed out the steering lever. The boys stepped back as they bowled past, taking the familiar road to the laboratory.

"I'll be interested to see what progress Mr. Malvern made on the chamber this week," she said to Tigg.

"I went yesterday, Lady. He's got it all constructed, and said 'e was waiting for you before 'e did a test ignition."

"How exciting! Does it look like the old chamber?"

"It's bigger. I could stand up in this 'un."

"Did he ... have any message for me?"

Tigg shook his head. "Just said 'e were impatient to see us Monday so's 'e could do the test and see wot adjustments we need to make."

Claire stifled a pang of disappointment. Of course he would say nothing to Tigg. And when they arrived at the laboratory and found him there, tinkering, he was his old self, breezy and self-deprecating and utterly unlike the man who had kissed her so passionately.

Which was all to the good, she thought as the baronial coach pulled to a stop, its horses stamping, and Lord James got out.

"Great Caesar's ghost," he said, gaping at her much as Jake and Lewis had done. "What in heaven's name have you got on?"

"A costume," she said, twirling like a ballerina. "Do you like it?"

"You look like an air pirate. Let those skirts down at once. Do you want His Royal Highness to see your knees?"

"They are covered in wool stockings, James. It is not likely he can see through them. Why, you are wearing hose yourself. What is the difference?"

He had chosen to go as an Elizabethan courtier, complete with white lace neck ruff and puffed and slashed pantaloons tied at the knee with ribbons. "The difference is that they are *your* knees."

"You are being illogical."

"And you are being intransigent."

"And you both look wonderful." Andrew moved between them. "With your masks on, I would not recognize either of you, which is the point of fancy dress, isn't it?"

"Just so," James said stiffly.

"So take your matching knees and go have a wonderful time. Lady Claire, I look forward to Monday, when we'll see what our contraption will do. Tigg, how fortuitous that you came. I could use your assistance, and then perhaps we'll go round the corner to the pub for a meat pie."

Tigg's face lit up. "Yes, sir. I'll just check the pilot flame on the landau, and be in in a tick."

It took all of the ride to Wellesley House for James to master his temper and speak civilly to her. There was no receiving line, of course, since it would not do to be recognized at the door, which allowed him to find a circulating waiter straightaway and secure two glasses of champagne. He knocked one back, found her a glass of punch, then drank the second one more slowly.

After that, he was ready to converse. And following that, to mingle.

Secure behind her mask, Claire smiled at the raised eyebrows and smothered gasps that her costume provoked. No Greek goddesses or china shepherdesses for her. The fact that her raiding rig was both sensational and utterly practical delighted her.

"Goodness. And what have we here?" said a fairy Claire assumed to be Titania, complete with glittering wings, in Julia Wellesley's unmistakable drawl.

"An air pirate, milady," Claire responded in her best airman's vernacular. "We moored t'yer roof an' gots our eyes on yer jewels."

Julia sniffed behind her silver mask. "What a pity everyone else's eyes are on your legs. Ah, well. Some people have no sense of propriety and are no doubt no better than they should be."

"Lord Robert Mount-Batting liked 'em well enough." Which was the truth. "Asked me for a waltz, 'e did." Which was almost the truth.

She had pretended to threaten him if he did not dance with her, and he had put up his hands, laughing, and surrendered. His name was on her card for the third waltz—which would never have happened if she had been in regular evening clothes. In her old life, she had been introduced to him at least five times and he could never remember who she was.

Julia whirled and pushed through the crowd, her wings raking the coiffures of passing ladies, and Claire resisted the urge to chuckle. Julia would no doubt be kinder if he had asked her to marry him when she expected him to, immediately following graduation.

"I say, well done," purred a voice behind her. Claire

turned to see the female equivalent of a Cowboy, complete with buckskin skirt, drover's coat, and a Colt repeating pistol strapped low on her hip. "It takes a woman with a spine to stand up to Julia Wellesley in her own ballroom."

Claire took a closer look at the merry black eyes behind the mask. "Peony Churchill?"

"The same. Jolly marvelous costume, Claire. I would never have recognized you. Even your walk and your carriage are different."

That was because she lived under no one's thumb nowadays. "How *did* you recognize me?" Heavens, if Peony could, then anybody could, and she would have to leave rather sooner than she'd planned.

"Your voice," Peony said simply. "Julia doesn't mix with the working classes, so she can't tell an imitation airman when she hears one. But I can."

"I shall have to do better, then. But tell me, why are you still in town? I thought you were going to the Canadas."

"I am. *Persephone* leaves on Saturday next, makes a stop in Paris, and I will be in New York by Wednesday night. From there we take another airship directly to Edmonton, and go by train to the mines up north."

"It sounds terribly exciting."

"It is. I do regret missing the new exhibitions coming to the Crystal Palace, though. The papers say they will include the most advanced engines ever invented."

"I shall write and describe them in detail, then."

"That would be wonderful. And put a few clippings in while you're at it. We shall get our mail care of the

Canadian Pacific Hotel in Edmonton."

"Expect one from me. Peony, is that pistol loaded?"

"Of course not, or I should be tempted to shoot Catherine Montrose. What about that magnificent device on your back?"

"Oh, yes, it's loaded. But Catherine is quite safe. It's for my own protection only."

Apropos of nothing, Peony said, "Is it really true you are engaged to Lord James Selwyn?"

"Yes," Claire said slowly.

"You sound as though you don't want to admit it."

"I—well, our engagement is—the circumstances are—"

A man materialized at Peony's elbow and bowed. "Oh, dear, this will be the second waltz. Goodbye, Cl— Mamzelle Air Pirate. I want you to tell me the end of that sentence in your letter."

"Safe travels," Claire said. Perhaps by then Peony would have forgotten.

By the time Lord Robert Mount-Batting appeared to claim his waltz, he was three sheets to the wind. If she had been a better dancer, she might have been tempted to lead, but as it was, she was forced to endure an embrace much closer than she would have preferred.

She had been perfectly right to wear her working clothes. The leather corselet protected her from roving hands as well as it did flying objects or certain kinds of weapons.

"Izzat a real gun?" he slurred, looking over her shoulder. "Where'd you get that?"

"I inherited it, and of course it's not real," she said, attempting to steer him away from a potted palm before he fell into it. "I imagine it's just painted ceramic."

"Looks real." He attempted to touch the barrel, and she gripped his hand firmly. "Who are you again?"

"If I told you that, sir, the unmasking at midnight would be dull indeed."

"Whole party's dull. Julia's angry with me. I ought to just go to the card room and stay there."

Claire perked up her ears. "There's a card room?"

"Course. Wanna play?"

Two hours later, Claire had cleaned out every man at her table using the very latest permutation of Cowboy Poker.

"I don't understand it," one man muttered—a knight with estates in Sussex, if she remembered correctly. "That hand just came out in the *Evening Standard* tonight. How is it possible for a female to know it already?"

Claire tucked her winnings in the wallet secured to her corselet by a chain, and wished the players good night. It wasn't until she was descending the steps to the ballroom again that she remembered the supper waltz, which she had promised to Lord James.

Oh, dear.

From the clatter in the dining room, it was over and done some time ago. She would apologize profusely, and consider it a bargain. After all, she had made enough tonight to pay for her first term at university, not counting books.

She collected a plate and arranged a nice selection of food on it, then turned to look for James. Ah, there he was, deep in conversation with Lord Wellesley. She would not interrupt that for the world. Instead, she was content to sit with three elderly ladies behind an arrangement of lilies and enjoy her dinner.

Once she had taken meals like this for granted. But no more. She appreciated every bite.

"—find it most distressing to think of," one of the ladies said.

"It's worse than that." Her companion did not seem to mind that a stranger had joined their party. With everyone masked, an odd sort of anonymity prevailed. "I heard she is to be admitted to a private sanitarium."

The curried prawns turned over in Claire's stomach. Had Dr. Craig been apprehended in the midst of leaving the country?

"Well, the family couldn't very well send her to Bedlam, could they?" Her companion tucked into her salad with enthusiasm. "She's the wife of an earl."

Claire resumed her dinner, relieved. Who on earth were they talking about?

"The poor girl. She's been going downhill ever since that precious child disappeared. I suppose it was only a matter of time before—"

"Oh, go ahead, Alethea. Just say 'before she made an attempt on her own life' and be done with it. We are not schoolgirls any longer."

Lady Dunsmuir. They were talking of Lady Dunsmuir, whose son had disappeared from the garden while his mother entertained a princess to tea. "She tried to take her own life?" Claire leaned forward. "When was this?"

"Two days ago. Such a pity. She's a shadow of what she once was, poor girl, and no hope of getting better. The only thing that will cure her is seeing her boy again, and that's not likely."

"Not after all the time that's passed." Alethea shook her head. "It's certain he is dead."

Alethea. This was Julia's grandmother, the Dowager Duchess, and a crony of Claire's great-aunts Beaton. Claire withdrew, and the ladies went on with their observations of the guests without her.

Poor Lady Dunsmuir. She should send a tube to her mother and let her know how things stood. They had been great friends once, before all the troubles. Perhaps Lady St. Ives would be able to give her some comfort.

Claire accepted another glass of punch from an obliging waiter and watched the dancers for a while, but then began to feel restive. She had never liked large crowds, or small talk, or the kind of empty social events that were more about being seen than about greeting friends. She was good at the latter, and abysmal at the former.

She would go out to the mews and see if she could find Gorse.

Her rig was designed for concealment. She slipped down a passage behind the roar of activity that was the kitchens, and into the rear courtyard. The sound of muffled wood on metal took her to a carriage house, where she found a man in livery beating a curve into what looked like a fender.

"Gorse!" She slipped off her mask and hooked it to her belt.

His jaw fell open and it was a moment before he could say, "Miss Claire!"

She was so happy to see him that she threw propriety to the winds and hugged him fiercely. He smelled of wool and engine oil and bay rum. "Are they treating you well here? Is this Lord Wellesley's four-piston Henley? What are you doing to it?"

"Slow down, miss, I haven't caught up with you yet. What are you doing here, and in that getup to boot?"

"It is a fancy-dress ball, Gorse. I had to wear something. But you didn't answer me. Are you well?"

"As well as can be expected, what with Silvie downalong."

"I was down to Gwynn Place this week with Lord James. Silvie is very well, and most of that hug I just gave you was from her."

"Lord James? Ah yes. I did hear a little news along that line. Are you happy, miss?"

"I'm very happy." Lord James had only a little to do with that, but Gorse did not need to know. "Thank you."

He gazed at her, then looked at the metal in his hands. "I'm trying to bend this fender back into shape. I'm afraid his Lordship isn't as handy with the engines as you are. He had an unfortunate tangle with a tree this afternoon."

"I hope it wasn't serious?"

"No, merely a brush, but enough to bend this here almost back to the fuselage." He gave it another whack with the wooden hammer wrapped in cloth.

"Let me help. If I hold it, then you can apply more pressure."

"But your ball, miss. Won't you be missed?"

"I hardly think so. I danced once, spoke to my hostess, played two hands of cards and won both, and had my supper. My social obligations are fulfilled. I would like to help."

They spent a very satisfying half hour repairing the fender, and then Claire got a personal tour of the four-piston's more sophisticated inner works.

"Do you still have the landau, miss? Ever since that night of the riots, I've thought of you and wondered how you were. I did get the one note, but that was all."

"I am very well. I live in Vauxhall Gardens, in a cottage by the river, and am governess to a number of orphan children."

"Are you now, miss?" His eyebrows rose. "And what does your lady mother have to say to that?"

"Plenty." She grinned at him. "But she is in Cornwall, so I cannot hear it."

"And his lordship? Mrs. Morven seems to think you will be living in Wilton Crescent again soon."

"His lordship may. I am going to the University of London to study engineering, as I've always told you I would."

"You're a singular young lady, miss," he said, admiringly. "I always thought folk underestimated you."

She only smiled. As the card players now knew, folks' underestimating a woman was often her greatest advantage.

17

On Monday, she sent a tube to Lady St. Ives tell her about the ball and the sad news about her old friend, omitting the part about the lecture James had read her on the way home. Apparently, the card players had not taken their losses like gentlemen.

Then she and Tigg drove to the laboratory with a sense of anticipation.

They found Andrew already there—did he sleep in the equipment loft?—and the chamber already humming. "Ah, I've been waiting for you," he said. "The coal is ready in the chamber. Tigg, will you do the honors?"

"Me, sir?" Tigg's eyes widened. "But you've been working at it all this time."

"With your assistance. Go on. Throw the switch. I must observe down at this end."

"Yes, sir."

He grasped the lever and jammed it upward with the flat of his hand. The chamber's hum increased, much the way the lightning rifle's did, and Claire clasped her hands at her breast. Would it work? Would the months of failed experiments now finally come to fruition?

A glow began to form in the glass chamber, surrounding the coal. "Yes!" she heard Andrew whisper. But before the word was fairly out of his mouth, the glow intensified, and then with a *pop* it went out.

She and Andrew looked at each other.

"Is that it, sir?" Tigg finally asked. "Should I shut it off?"

"Yes. Let me inspect the coal."

He unscrewed the cowling and the bottom of the chamber lowered, revealing coal that looked very much like ... coal.

Andrew touched it. Examined it. Took it over to a microscope and gazed at it under the magnifying lenses. Then he sat rather abruptly on the unused chair.

Claire couldn't hold back another second. "Well?"

"Nothing. As far as I can see, the coal is completely unchanged."

"Try it again. Perhaps it needs more than one treatment."

They tried again. And again. And by noon, Claire could bear it no longer, and made Andrew stop. "Mr. Malvern, please. You will do yourself harm. It is clear that there is some error in our calculations."

In reply, he threw the innocent coal so hard against the wall of the warehouse that it bounced halfway back again. "I don't understand. Your drawings were perfect. Everything that Doctor Craig said was necessary is in that chamber. What did I do wrong?"

"We will find the error," she assured him. "We must apply our minds to it until we do."

They spent the rest of the afternoon on it, and when she and Tigg returned to the cottage, the two of them disassembled the lightning rifle and studied the pieces. "It's the same, Lady," Tigg said. "The chamber is just a bigger version of your glass globe, 'ere. The cell is the same—I've looked at it often enough."

Claire pushed her hair off her hot forehead. "We can do no more tonight. Let us reassemble it so that Granny Protheroe can bring in our tea. Perhaps the answer will take us unawares."

After supper, Claire took her usual spot in the garden, Willie on her lap, the two of them watching the chickens nibbling the last few bites of grass while the walking coop stumped over to its resting place next to the back porch.

She gazed at the machine, then turned and called in the open door, "Lizzie? Will you come here a moment?"

Lizzie came reluctantly, having just discovered a cache of cookies. She brought some with her and offered one to Claire and one to Willie. "Wotcher want, Lady?"

"Thank you, dear." She indicated the coop. "I've been looking at your coop and observing that it doesn't have the usual mechanisms to power the legs. Was that an improvement made by Doctor Craig?"

Lizzie nodded. "She said the steam engine wot went with these legs was too big for our coop, so she made us one of 'er cells, like in the lightning rifle."

"Did she, now. That was clever. I'm surprised she remembered how, after all those years."

"Me, too. But it don't work right away. Jake an' Lewis made us one o' them little engines what power the firelamps, only bigger. That gets it goin'."

"Why should that make a difference?"

"Dunno." The child finished off her cookie with relish. "But it does. It don't start to glow without the coop movin' a bit first."

Moving.

Kineticks.

The rifle was usually in motion when she used it.

Great Caesar's ghost.

She set Willie on his feet and seized Lizzie in a hug that made her gasp. "That's it! You have solved it, you brilliant child—you and Jake and Lewis. Oh, I foresee many roasts of beef and Yorkshire puddings in this house in the future. Run and get Tigg. We are going back to the laboratory immediately."

Willie roared at this disruption in their evening routine. He clung to her skirts as she fetched her hat and her engineering notebook, and even as she prepared to climb into the landau, he wept and clutched her legs through the practical twill.

Finally Tigg said, "Come on, old man. 'Op in and you shall go with us."

He subsided in the passenger seat on Tigg's lap, hiccupping and sniffling, his hand twisted in Claire's skirt.

Without the busy day's traffic, they reached the laboratory in record time, only to find it locked and empty.

"'E's likely gone 'ome, Lady," Tigg said. "Do you know where he lives?"

Claire had not filed hundreds of papers without noticing that some had gone to his home address. The wind of their going practically lifted off her hat as they crossed the Blackfriars Bridge and turned left on the Victoria Embankment, then headed north for Russell Square in Bloomsbury.

She pulled to a stop in front of a neat row house with a shiny black door. The son of a policeman and a cook had done well for himself—all due to his wits and ambition. Warm yellow light glowed from the windows, and as Claire shut down the landau's boiler, she belatedly wondered if he might have company.

Never mind. This was too important to sleep on. "Come along, boys."

Andrew answered the knocker in slack-jawed surprise. "Claire! And Tigg and Willie. What—is everything all right?"

"More than all right," she assured him. "We have a discovery we must share with you immediately. It will not wait until morning."

"Come in." He led them into a cozy parlor, then to a dining room the size of a handkerchief, where the table was set for two. A woman rose, setting her napkin aside. "Lady Claire Trevelyan, may I present my mother, Mrs. Jane Malvern. Mother, this is my laboratory assistant, of whom we were just speaking."

Mrs. Malvern began to dip into a curtsey, but Claire

forestalled her with a handshake. "I'm so happy to meet you. And these are my charges, Tigg and young Willie."

Willie sidled out from behind Claire's skirts and both he and Tigg bowed. Bless their hearts, how proud she was of their manners.

Mrs. Malvern stared at the boys, her greeting dying on her lips when Claire turned in excitement to Andrew. "Please sit and continue with your dinner. Mr. Malvern, we—that is, Lizzie and Jake and Lewis and Doctor Craig—have made the most astonishing discovery. It was in front of me all the time and I did not see it until this evening."

"Claire, the suspense is killing me." Andrew did not pick up his knife and fork.

"It is simply this—we are using *kinetick* energy now. Movement. Andrew, *the chamber must be in motion* in order for the cell to work."

"What?"

"Lizzie pointed the anomaly out to me not half an hour ago. Doctor Craig installed a lightning cell in our walking coop. But it won't activate until a preliminary engine—which we designed for a project not long ago—gets the coop in motion. *Kineticks*, Andrew. We have been predicating everything on *electricks*. No wonder we made such an error."

"Great Caesar's ghost."

"My sentiments exactly." She laid her engineering notebook on the table. "We must modify the chamber again."

"I agree. Mother, did you hear? Such a breakthrough! I almost want to—"

"Lady Claire." Mrs. Malvern's face had gone as white as the table linens. "Who is this child?"

It took a moment for Claire's mind to move from the aether of science to the room in which she sat. "Which child?" Tigg was seated at the end of the table, looking rather longingly at the filet of plaice on the plates of the others, though Claire knew for a fact he had had two helpings of stew at home. Willie had not taken a chair at all, preferring instead to stand next to hers, regarding everything in this strange household from within the circle of her left arm.

"The younger."

"Why, this is Willie. Did I not introduce him?"

"You did. What I want to know is, where did he come from?"

"Mother, this is hardly the time. Lady Claire and I must—"

"You and Lady Claire must listen to me. *Where did this child come from?*"

Claire gaped at her blankly. What was she to say when she had absolutely no idea?

Tigg stirred in his chair. "'E was wiv—with us when the Lady came to us, mum. 'E brought 'er to us, you might say."

"And where did you find him?"

Tigg screwed up his face with the effort to remember. "It was that 'ot summer a couple of years back. Snou—er, Mr. McTavish, the Lady's secretary, 'ad been to the river with some of our mates to swim and when 'e came 'ome, Willie was with him."

"The river. Two years ago."

"Yes'm. Thereabouts."

"Mother, what has come over you?" Andrew asked. "What is all this about?"

"Simply this," she said. "Two years ago, a three-year-old boy was stolen from a garden while his nurse slept. A boy with brown hair in a widow's peak like his father's, and big blue eyes like his mother's. A boy for whom I used to make sugar cookies shaped like stars, because they were his favorite."

To Claire's astonishment, Willie grinned at the older woman, his dimpled chin barely level with the tabletop as he stood pressed against her. Then he pushed away, ducked under the table to the other woman's place, and flung himself into her lap. Mrs. Malvern gasped as she tried to hold back a sob, gathering him into her arms as she spoke in a voice close to tears.

"A boy whose name is Lord Wilberforce Albert John Dunsmuir, Viscount Hatley, and Baron Craigdarroch." With each syllable she gave him a tiny shake, as if impressing them into his memory, though her voice broke. "The son of Lord and Lady Dunsmuir, who have been looking for him without ceasing these two long and empty years."

18

It was nearly ten o'clock, and Claire wondered if Lord Dunsmuir would have them thrown out of his library as charlatans. "They have had to deal with all manner of criminals parading boys in front of them, every one trained to pretend he was a lord," Jane Malvern told them in a low voice. "But young Willie is no pretender. I would know those eyes anywhere."

A patter of footsteps sounded on the grand staircase of Hatley House, the Dunsmuirs' town house bordering on Regents' Park. Somewhere above, a man's stifled voice said, "Davina, no. You will do yourself harm. Please, let me—"

With a rustle of silk, a woman appeared in the door of the library in a dressing gown, breathing hard. "Mrs.

Malvern," she said. "You would not trifle with—please tell me—" Her wide blue gaze fell on Willie, who until that moment had been pressed against Claire's side while she knelt, her arm around his shoulders.

She distinctly heard Willie suck in a great breath, and in the next moment he had bounded across the room, the woman had flung herself to her knees and opened her arms, and mother and son both burst into tears as they clutched each other in a bear hug.

Lord Dunsmuir, his shirt collar open and his feet bare, finally reached the library. "Is it—? Davina—?"

"Yes, milord, it is," Mrs. Malvern said, dabbing at her eyes with an embroidered handkerchief. "It is really your boy, after all this time."

"But how—? How did you—?"

The poor man did not seem able to complete a sentence. Finally he abandoned the attempt altogether and joined his wife and son on the floor, manfully attempting to keep his tears back, and failing utterly.

Willie looked at Claire over his parents' shoulders. "Mama and papa," he said, clear as day, beaming with such happiness that Claire came near to tears herself.

"Yes, darling," she said. "Your mama and papa, at last."

After several more minutes, the earl finally collected himself enough to speak coherently. "Mrs. Malvern, you must tell us how this—this miracle came to pass."

"I think that story belongs to Lady Claire, milord. She has been acting in a mother's place for many weeks, I think."

"Lady Claire?" For the first time, the earl seemed to

notice that there were a number of additional people in the quiet, carpeted room.

"Yes, my lord," Claire said. "I am Claire Trevelyan, daughter of the late Viscount and Lady St. Ives."

"You are Vivyan and Flora's daughter?" he said blankly. "How did you come to be acquainted with our cook—not to mention my boy?"

"I am Andrew Malvern's laboratory assistant," she said, blithely ignoring his lordship's look of shock and sticking to the facts. "After my family's ruin, I was forced to seek employment. In the course of that effort, I met a group of orphans who eventually came under my care. Your son was one of them. But I must tell you, my lord, I have been caring for Willie since the beginning of the summer, and not once have I heard him speak. The other children told me he had been struck dumb—some think it was by an early trauma. To the best of my knowledge, the words he just said are the first to cross his lips in two years."

The countess looked into Willie's eyes. "Is it true, my darling?" she asked softly. "Is what she says true?"

"Yeth," he said, and Claire smiled to realize that his little lordship lisped. "They thaid they'd kill me."

"Dear God." The countess hugged him to her breast again.

"Thnouts ith my friend. He thaved me from the bad men." He looked back at Claire. "I love the Lady, Mama. Can she thtay with uth?"

Claire's eyes filled with tears again as she knelt next to them. "This is your home again, my dear one, and my home is in the cottage. But we will see each other often, I promise. Just because you have come home does not mean you can neglect your studies in reading and mathematics."

"You have been teaching him?" Lady Davina asked.

"She teaches us all, milady," Tigg piped up. "I can read now, and do sums, I'm Mr. Malvern's assistant too."

The countess blinked at him. "My goodness. I have more to be grateful for than I ever dreamed."

The earl got to his feet. "This is not the time, but by all I hold dear, I will find the miscreants who took my boy, and see them in gaol. Perhaps when it is convenient I could speak to this ...?" He gazed inquiringly at Claire.

"Snouts? He means Mr. McTavish, my secretary, whose nose, regrettably, is a source of great fun for the boys." She had no doubt that *convenient* to the earl meant *immediately, if not sooner.* "Perhaps we might call tomorrow afternoon, if you are at home?"

The countess stood, and Claire found herself in a fierce embrace. "We are always at home to you—to you all. I can never, ever repay you for bringing my boy home to me."

"My wife is right," Lord Dunsmuir said. "If there is anything any of you need, anything I can do, you have merely to name it, and it will be done instantly."

"Your lordship is very kind," Claire said. "But at the moment, I have all I need."

"As do I," Andrew said. "And my mother lacks for nothing."

"But if at any time your situation should change,"

the earl told them, "any of you, even your secretary or this young man here—"

"That'th Tigg," his son informed him. "He'th my friend, too."

The earl acknowledged Tigg with a nod, one man to another. "—I wish to be the one to assist. I mean it. No matter what it is, it cannot be enough to equal my gratitude."

The moment was a good one to exercise delicacy, and Claire and Andrew took their leave. Willie looked confused, and made to go with her, but she knelt and said, "No, darling. Your mama wishes to tuck you into your very own bed, and kiss you good-night. How lovely that will be!"

"You will come back, Lady?"

"Of course. Your papa and I and Snouts are to have a visit tomorrow afternoon, so you will see us then."

"Promith?"

"Cross my heart." And she did so.

Only then was he satisfied, and the little group took their leave.

In the landau once again, bowling down the side of Russell Square, an emotionally drained silence reigned until Tigg said, in wondering tones, "Wilberforce. Huh. Wonder if he expects us to call 'im that now?"

"Oh, no," Andrew said. "You must address him as *Lord* Wilberforce. Or Viscount Hatley."

Tigg made a rude noise. "Not bleedin' likely. 'E's our Willie, no matter what."

"I imagine he will be perfectly happy to be known as Willie to his friends," Mrs. Malvern put in. "And you certainly have a friend for life in his lordship. Goodness gracious me, what a night it has been!"

What a night, indeed. Claire realized with a sense of shock that she had not thought of the chamber or of kineticks or science at all in more than three hours. And somehow, when she remembered the joy that had filled that library, it seemed only right.

The Evening Standard
August 26

KIDNAPPED VISCOUNT RETURNS

In a turn of events straight from the pages of a penny dreadful, the young Viscount Hatley, stolen from the garden of Hatley House two years ago while his nanny slept, has been restored to the arms of his joyful parents.

According to a source close to the family, Lord and Lady Dunsmuir were summoned from their beds in the middle of the night to find a group of Good Samaritans—as yet unnamed—with a young boy they claimed to be Lord Wilberforce. As our readers are aware, the Dunsmuirs have been summoned to many such meetings, all of which have been proven to be the work of confidence men attempting to pass off urchins and alley mice as the missing lord.

SHELLEY ADINA

But the credentials of these unnamed angels appear to have been bona fide, because this morning Lord and Lady Dunsmuir announced to their callers that their son had been returned. Little is known of the harrowing events of his captivity, save that he was sworn to silence on pain of death. The boy has been mute for two years, and only the sight of his mother loosened his tongue once more.

Lord Dunsmuir has posted a reward of 100 pounds for any information leading to the capture of his son's kidnappers, with a further 100 pounds due when they are proven guilty and sentenced to gaol or transport.

The editors of this newspaper join our readers in thanking Providence for the return of the young viscount, and offer our hopes that his ordeal will soon be forgotten in the joy of his return to the family circle.

19

"'E's only been gone two days and I miss 'im already."

Tigg finished with the last of the screws on a contraption that, if Claire had to say so herself, was fairly ingenious. Andrew had wasted no time in another trip to the manufactory, and between the two of them, they had created a sort of metal hammock that would set the chamber in motion. Once the cell was activated, the hammock could be locked in place so that the ignition process could occur with some precision in the chamber itself.

"He's not really gone, you know," Claire assured him. "His lordship has said we may visit at any time, with no restrictions."

"It won't be the same, though. 'E won't be able to

come and see us, will 'e?"

"I shall ask. The Mopsies miss him, too, and the chickens will forget who he is if he does not come within two weeks. But we must understand if Lord and Lady Dunsmuir are not quite prepared to let him out of their sight. Not this soon, at any rate."

"Are we ready out there?" Andrew called from behind the control apparatus, where he was tinkering with gears.

Tigg scrambled down and put his screwdriver and mallet away carefully in a leather case that appeared to be rather new. "Yes, sir," he called.

"Come on over, then, and man the switches."

This time the ignition procedure was more complicated. Tigg set the hammock in motion with one switch, and Andrew raised his arm to signify that the cell had begun to glow. With his other hand, Andrew brought his goggles down to cover his eyes, and motioned for Claire to do the same. When the hum in the chamber reached a pitch that satisfied him, Andrew's arm swung down sharply and Tigg rammed the control lever all the way up. A blinding light flashed in the chamber—bright as the bolt that had killed Lightning Luke—engulfing the pile of coal. Again, Claire saw the tendrils of power flicker and touch the chunks of coal, delicate as a spider climbing from top to bottom, before the current dissipated and the chamber settled into inactivity once more.

A plume of smoke rose from the coal and was whisked away by the air flowing through the chamber and out through a brass pipe that led out of doors.

Once again, Tigg lowered the cowling and Andrew examined the coal in his heavily gloved hands. He looked up at Claire. "This does not look like the coal we began with."

"I should say not. All the pieces are fused together."

"This won't fit under the microscope, and it's hot—I must put it down. We shall have to field test it. Tigg, where's your mallet?"

"Here, sir."

A smart tap on the coal produced a clink rather like metal hitting metal.

"Claire, Tigg, this is a good sign," Andrew breathed. "It is hard, is it not? I'm not just imagining it because I want it to be so?"

"Let me, sir."

Tigg tapped all around the sample, careful not to let it touch his hands. "It's glowing hot, sir, but it doesn't burn. How can that be?"

"I suppose if we heated a diamond, the result would be the same. Now, come upstairs. We shall give it another test. The bonfire I lit in the stove should be hot coals by now."

He carried the sample upstairs in a metal pan, and with the tongs, put it on the thick bed of red-hot coals in the stove. Every half hour, he checked its progress, dictating the results over his shoulder to Claire.

She and Tigg had their lunch, and then she went shopping, since the skirts she had left Wilton Crescent with were getting rather well used. At four she returned to collect Tigg, and found them both upstairs.

Andrew closed the stove door and wiped the perspiration from his forehead. A streak of coal lay upon his cheek, and Claire resisted the urge to use her handkerchief to wipe it away. "Eight hours, and it's still burning. This is miraculous."

"Is it safe to say it worked, sir?" Tigg asked.

"I don't mind confessing to you that I have failed so many times I hardly dare say whether something is working or not. We shall not know for certain until we have a large sample we can test in an actual train. But for now, I will venture to say it looks promising, Tigg. Very, very promising." He looked up at Claire and stood, dusting off the knees of his trousers under the heavy leather apron. "And it would not have happened were it not for all of you. Claire, I shall write that letter to the university board of regents this very night."

"But I did not invent the cell, Mr. Malvern. Doctor Craig should have the credit."

"Doctor Craig shall, when we call a press conference and announce it to the world. But it was not she who designed that movable truss, was it, to create the initial motion? It was not she who made the connection between the walking coop—which I still want to see sometime, by the way—and my ignition chamber. It was you. And believe me, the board shall hear about it from me."

"Thank you, Mr. Malvern."

"Claire, I think we know each other well enough now for you to call me by my Christian name."

"Thank you, Andrew," she said softly.

She didn't mean to look at him, then. But when he said nothing, she raised her head to see if something was wrong ... and she saw his face.

The naked longing. The admiration. The softness in his eyes.

She blushed, and felt the heat searing her cheeks in all its blotchy unattractiveness. And then Tigg spoke, shattering the spell into fragments.

"I'll go shovel a bigger load into the chamber, then, shall I, sir?"

"Yes, thank you, Tigg. I'll be down in a moment."

The boy clattered downstairs, but Andrew did not move. And until he did, Claire was trapped between him and the desk.

"I meant it, Claire. I shall write your letter tonight ... if you still plan to use it."

"Of course I do. Without a letter of recommendation from a member of the Royal Society of Engineers, I cannot apply to the engineering program. You know that."

"I do, and I also know that you and James came to an understanding while you were down in Cornwall."

"Is that so?"

"An autumn wedding, he tells me, which under normal circumstances would preclude a university career."

"My circumstances are hardly normal."

"Are you going to go through with it?"

She had managed to bury her conversation with James on the beach under larger concerns, except for the times when the thought of it woke her in the middle of the night. "He and my mother have come to an understanding," she managed at last. "I shall be eighteen in October, but until then, legally I am under my mother's control."

"Are they trying to force you?" His fists clenched.

She drew herself up. "No one can force me. I just wish I knew which was the best course. In some ways he is a good match—"

A muscle twitched in his jaw. "Barons usually are."

"I didn't mean in that way. We both have strong personalities and inflexible wills, which may or may not be a good thing. We have a similar upbringing, and a place in society." She paused. "We share an interest in steam engines and trains."

"Marriages have been based on less," he allowed.

"But—" She gazed at him, beseeching.

"But ...?"

"You kissed me," she whispered.

Now he flushed as deeply as she. "We were to forget that," he said. "It was dishonorable of me to do it, and dishonorable of you to speak of it again."

"But it happened. And it changed everything."

"It did?" Somehow, without her realizing it, she had come to stand in front of him. He reached out to grip her upper arms. "Claire, it was foolish and wrong and we must both forget it."

"Must we? Can we?"

For a moment, entire futures hung in the balance. In those seconds of loaded silence, Claire searched his face, seeing the truth: that with one word, her life and his could change.

And then the door banged downstairs and James's voice boomed through the laboratory. "Andrew? I got your tube. Is it really true? Do we have a working prototype at last?"

And the moment scattered into noise and confusion, like a flock of startled pigeons.

Andrew released her and went downstairs, and while he explained the mechanics of the new chamber and Tigg set it in motion, Claire filed papers and cleaned out cabinet drawers as if her life depended on it. It wasn't until she heard her name mentioned repeatedly that she judged it safe to come down, and by then, James was absorbed in the spectacle of the kinetick charge doing its work on the coal in the chamber.

When the sample lay cooling in the metal pan, James realized that Claire was standing with them.

"I can hardly believe it," he said. "Am I to understand that we owe this breakthrough to you?"

"Not me," she said. "To Lizzie and Lewis and—and others."

"I refuse to believe that a gang of uneducated alley mice could have come up with this device."

"James, please do not call them that. They are far from uneducated."

"Their names will not be going on the patent application."

"Let's not get ahead of ourselves," Andrew said hastily. "James, the first sample we created has been burning for eight hours—nearly nine, now. If the burn time is consistent, our next step is to test the samples in a steam locomotive."

"I shall send a tube immediately to Ross Stephenson." James paused, and Claire could practically see his mind leaping ahead. "If he can arrange to put a train at our disposal, we could travel with the samples to Birmingham, perhaps as soon as the day after tomorrow. Claire, can you be ready to travel again at such short notice?"

"Travel?" she said blankly. "To Birmingham? Me?"

"You hold shares in the Midlands Railroad, don't you?" he asked with some asperity. "Ross Stephenson is the chairman, and it is only fitting that as my fiancée you should meet him at some point. If this chamber really works, our association could be of some duration."

"But what about the—"

"No children this time. It is one thing to take a menagerie down to Cornwall to your family estate. It is quite another to take them to a business meeting with a very influential industrialist."

"James, I can't possibly—"

"Give it some thought. I hope you will see the benefits of the plan, particularly if your name is to be recorded on the patent."

"That should be a given whether she goes or not," Andrew put in.

"And it just occurred to me," James went on without acknowledging his partner, "that if you are looking for letters of recommendation, what better signature to have on such a letter than Ross Stephenson's? He is, after all, a past president of the Royal Society."

Claire had not known that. But what was this talk of letters when the last she had heard, she was to be married to him practically the day after she turned eighteen? Was he toying with her? Or had he reconsidered his high-handed plan?

She resisted the compulsion to look at Andrew.

And then she realized what she was in for.

A trip to Birmingham, whether by airship or steam train, in the company of both men—one to whom she was engaged but had very conflicted feelings for, and one for whom her feelings were not in the least conflicted, but who was barred to her forever by her own actions.

Oh, dear.

The coal sample was not the only thing, it seemed, to be placed in a most incendiary position.

20

The test locomotive, it turned out, would require a ton of the experimental coal in its tender, so the chamber was set to work in fifty-pound increments, around the clock. Tigg trained Snouts and Jake to take alternating shifts, and by late Thursday, the entire amount had been produced and sent to the rail yard in an enormous, lumbering steam dray. Mr. Stephenson had a locomotive at Euston Station that was scheduled to deadhead back to Birmingham on Friday, so they were instructed to conduct the experiment on the way.

He attached two first-class salon cars and a dining car with his compliments.

Clearly, there were advantages to hobnobbing with railroad men. Claire wondered whether becoming socially acquainted with the heads of airship companies might not produce a similar result. She made a mental note to instruct Mr. Arundel to buy stock in *Persephone* to begin with, and in the Albion Airship Company, which owned the domestic vessels serving all of England. What a pity Peony had already sailed—Claire would bet a gold guinea that the Churchills were socially acquainted with that raffish lot, the Cunards.

James strode down the platform to where Claire stood next to the tender, watching Andrew and Tigg briefing the fireman on the properties of the experimental coal.

"I thought I said there were to be no children on this trip," he said, without so much as a *Good morning, dear.*

"Tigg is not a child," she replied with some spirit. "He is Mr. Malvern's assistant, and has been since the chamber was re-invented."

"*You* are his assistant."

"I am, but Tigg is much more willing to leap about loading chambers and getting covered in coal dust than I am. He thrives on it, in fact." As she spoke, Tigg was hunkered down next to the fireman, showing him the properties of the new coal while Andrew told him how they expected the substance to behave once they were under way.

"Once again you have outwitted me."

She couldn't tell if he meant to be sarcastic or not. The smile that might have accompanied such a statement was missing entirely. "I have not. Tigg is a necessary part of this enterprise—certainly more necessary than I. I am merely window dressing."

"I disagree. There are more parts to this enterprise, as you call it, than the merely mechanical. There is a social element, too."

"Which brings me to the second part of Tigg's usefulness. It would be dreadfully improper for your fiancée to travel with you unchaperoned, in the company of another man. If I travel as Tigg's governess, then no tongues will wag."

"That boy needs no governess."

"My point exactly. He is no child. However, the social niceties must be preserved."

Having hoisted him with his own petard, she gave him a sunny smile and made her way to the salon car, where her traveling case and engineering notebook rested next to a comfortable chair. A tea service had already been laid out, but she waited until the whistle blew and the train jerked into motion before she poured. Some time later, James, Andrew, and Tigg found her, the latter two ravenously hungry.

"A ton of untreated coal will take us about forty miles," Andrew said between mouthfuls of egg salad. "I am exceedingly anxious to see what the new material will do. James, we shall have to think of a name for it. *New material* and *treated coal* are cumbersome, to say the least."

"Kinetick coal?" Tigg suggested.

"Malvernite," Claire said. What a pity Dr. Craig's involvement could not be known. *Craig coal* had an interesting ring to it.

"Selwynite." Andrew snapped his fingers. "That's it."

"Now, now," James said, clearly pleased and trying not to show it, "let's not get ahead of ourselves. We wouldn't want the champagne christening to cause the ship to sink, would we?"

At about the forty-mile mark, Claire could see Andrew and James becoming increasingly restive. At fifty miles, they could stand it no longer, and went forward to the tender.

Sixty miles. No news.

Seventy. And eighty. Good heavens. Had they forgotten that she was along for the ride, and had as much interest in the project as any of them? She closed her notebook and packed it away, and located her hat. New skirt or not, danger notwithstanding, she would go forward and find out what was going on.

At eighty-five miles, Tigg burst through the salon doors. "Lady! It works!"

"It's about time someone gave me some news. I was just about to go forward myself."

"Mr. Malvern sent me to tell you. One ton of our coal 'as taken this train eighty-five miles. We're almost to Birmingham!"

"Heavens. Let us go forward, Tigg, at once."

"No, Lady, they're right behind me. Lord James says 'e has champagne in his traveling case. D'you think 'e'll let me 'ave some?"

In the ensuing celebration, Tigg was allowed approximately a thimbleful of champagne—"Oy," he said, wrinkling his nose, "I dunno wot the fuss is about— there's nuffink to that stuff." By the time they reached Curzon Street Station, James was in fine fettle.

He leaped from the salon car the moment it had fairly halted at the platform, and vigorously shook the hand of the man waiting there with his entourage.

"Claire, may I present Ross Stephenson, chairman of the Midlands Railroad. Ross, this is my fiancée, Lady Claire Trevelyan."

"How do you do?" Claire extended a gloved hand to the man, who shook it with rather more force than Claire expected.

"A pleasure to meet you, Lady Claire," he said, as bluff as the Prince of Wales himself and at least as expensively dressed. His coat was collared in fox, though it was a warm day, and its facings were velvet. His beaver top hat gleamed with daily brushing, and Claire could practically see reflections in his shoes. "My wife will be delighted to make your acquaintance also. If you will excuse me, I will take his lordship and Mr. Malvern off your hands and down to my offices. My second landau—a six-piston Delage—is waiting to take you out to the house."

"But I wish to go along and hear the results."

He looked flummoxed, and glanced at James. "Business talk. No-ho, my dear, it would bore you to bits. Mrs. Stephenson—Lady Elizabeth Drummond as was—will have refreshments waiting for you before we dress for dinner."

Now it was her turn to glance at James. "Mr. Stephenson, it is hardly likely I would be bored by the results of my own—"

"Now, Claire," James said in a low tone, attempting to lead her away from the group. "Ross Stephenson is a bit old-fashioned. I've kept his knowledge of our arrangements fairly simple so that—"

She cut him off. "Do you mean to tell me he does not know of my involvement?"

"That is correct."

She tried to keep her voice low and her face pleasant, in case anyone watching should think they were actually having a quarrel. "Then you must inform him of the truth. It is terribly rude to allow him to labor under a misconception."

"As I said, he's old-fashioned. In his mind, women belong in the ballroom, not the laboratory."

"It is time he was educated."

"It is not the time. Claire, you are making a scene."

"A scene!" He had no idea of the kind of scene she could make. "Do you ever plan to tell him the truth?"

"Of course, dear, just as soon as the contracts are signed. His opinion of a woman's place is of no consequence anyway. In the larger scheme, it is your name going on the patent."

"But James, if he is to give me a letter of recommendation, he must know of my involvement, to the last line and measurement!"

"All in good time, dear. First we must get his commitment to the venture in writing. Everything else will follow from that."

She didn't know whether to be mollified or not. But she did know one thing: It was ridiculous that James and Andrew should go off in one gleaming steam landau while she and Tigg were taken out into the countryside in another like a pair of babies in a pram.

Lady Elizabeth turned out to be the widow of an impoverished lord, and had received Mr. Stephenson's courtship with open arms. His grown children had not needed her guidance as a parent, but they needed her cachet as they made their debuts in London, and held her in some affection as a result.

Claire endured yet another description of the daughter's ballgowns and wondered where on earth the men had got to. If they didn't come and save her from this poor woman, she would grab Tigg and run screaming down the mile-long drive. That young man had found a book in the library, and was on the couch opposite, poring over drawings of locomotives and sounding out the words and figures, his lips moving silently.

Lucky Tigg. At least he had something of interest to occupy his mind.

At last came the crunch of gravel in the sweep outside, and Lady Elizabeth smiled brightly. "This will be Ross and dear Lord James. I do hope they have enjoyed themselves together."

"I am quite sure they have."

The men came in then, all bonhomie and full of plans for the future. In her days at St. Cecelia's Academy for Young Ladies, Claire had endured plenty of moments when she had felt shut out and ignored. But it hadn't been like this. It was one thing to be excluded from a discussion of who would partner whom when the Heathbourne boys came across the square for a joint dance class. It was quite another to be excluded from a discussion of her own invention.

On purpose. By the man who was supposed to hold

her in such esteem.

Any tender feelings that might have taken root during his confession on the beach were rapidly being blasted to ruin with every course during the interminable dinner. She was thankful Tigg had gone away with the upstairs maid to supper in the unused nursery with his book and then bed. He had tumbled to what was going on before ten minutes had passed, and his natural instinct to right what he saw as a terrible misunderstanding would get him into more trouble than Claire was willing to allow.

When the men finally joined her and Lady Elizabeth in the drawing room after their brandy, she was barely able to be civil, and Lady Elizabeth had actually gone so far as to ask gently if she were suffering from a headache.

After that, Claire pulled herself together. Her hostess did not deserve her bad temper. She made an extra effort to be smiling and kind, to the point that Lady Elizabeth was charmed to forgetfulness and would afterward to refer to her as "Lady Claire, that dear child, such a pity."

Mr. Stephenson poured cognac into a glass and handed it to Lord James. "A toast, my friend, to our success. I'll come down with you tomorrow and see this chamber in action. Then we'll want to build a prototype at my ironworks."

"After the contracts are signed," James put in.

"Of course, of course, old man." James accepted the glass and toasted his host with it.

Andrew took one as well. "Here's a thought for both of you. The Royal Society has been buzzing for days about the new exhibits going in at the Crystal Palace. I submit that our chamber is at least as ground-breaking as any of those engines. Why don't we enter it?"

Claire drew in a breath. Dr. Craig's device—her own moving truss—both working together in an environment where every scientist in the city could see it ... what a grand opportunity to reveal the inventors of both! Even without Mr. Stephenson's letter of recommendation, the fact that she had an exhibit in the Crystal Palace would guarantee her a seat in the engineering program. Nothing could trump that.

She could barely keep her seat on the Nile green brocade settee.

"That's a capital idea," Mr. Stephenson said. "I thought you were a man of science, Mr. Malvern, but I see you are adept at the public side, as well."

"Not really," Andrew said modestly. "But I do know that having an exhibit in the Crystal Palace will raise the visibility of our device throughout England ... and across the ocean."

Mr. Stephenson snorted. "If by that you mean the Americas, I wouldn't worry about them. They're so busy scrambling to keep up with us that they have no time to develop anything original on their own."

"They do pay well, though," Andrew said. "Did you hear that they have tempted Count Zeppelin to build a shipyards at a place called Lakehurst, New Jersey, so that the lords of industry will have access to domestic airships?"

"I did not hear that," Mr. Stephenson replied. "Avery Cunard will not appreciate his monopoly being broken by Prince Albert's countrymen, no-ho, not one bit."

"In any case, it is said to be the single largest international deal to be signed since our glorious Queen came to the throne."

Lady Elizabeth looked pained. "Must we speak of money? Come, Mr. Stephenson, gentlemen. Let us turn to more civilized topics."

The lady had exchanged a title for a fortune. Perhaps she was sensitive on the subject. Claire wished she had not spoken, though. Her father had never discussed such interesting subjects at home, and now that she was being exposed to them when she was with Andrew and James, she was developing quite a taste for them.

German-designed airships to be built in the Americas. Fascinating.

"I believe you should exhibit the chamber at the Crystal Palace," she said. "The timing could not be better. Were you not just telling me on the journey, James, that the exhibit should come first, and then, when excitement is at its highest pitch, the announcement of your joint venture with Mr. Stephenson could be made." She smiled at him so sweetly that sugar crystals practically formed in the air.

Mr. Stephenson clapped James on the back and laughed. "O-ho, you have it all planned out, like the man of vision I knew you to be."

James shot Claire a look that promised they would be revisiting the "women should be seen and not heard" edict later on. "It is kind of you to remind me, dear. Not only will we gain visibility for the device, as Andrew suggests, but the Midlands Railway Company will be seen as leading the van of progress when it adopts a new technology."

"Capital!" Mr. Stephenson beamed at them all, and Claire prevented herself with difficulty from rolling her eyes.

After that, of course, their host was feeling expansive enough to allow his wife to play a tune or two on the piano. Claire declined his invitation, however. Playing and singing were not talents she was willing to inflict on the present company. If he were to suggest target practice, that would be a different matter, but it did not seem likely.

Though the public rooms were lighted with electricks, the upper floors were not, so the guests were given lamps to light their way to bed. James stopped Claire outside the door to her room as Andrew passed them. "Good night, Claire. James. We will have an early start tomorrow, so I wish you a good rest."

"Thank you," Claire said. *Stay*, her heart cried. *Talk to me. Reassure me that James will not ride roughshod over both of us. Hold me.*

"A word, dear, if you are not too tired?"

She silenced the longing inside and turned to her fiancé. "Here, in the passage?"

"Certainly not. In here."

"James, this is my room."

"I am aware of that. It will offer us some privacy."

"That would not be proper, engaged or not. What would our hostess say?"

"Oh, for heaven's sake. In this one, then."

HER OWN DEVICES

At the top of the stairs was a small room fitted out with bookshelves and a couple of chairs. The titles were those Claire had read in her childhood. Perhaps the first Mrs. Stephenson had sat here and read stories to her children at bedtime. In any case, it would do for the present.

"If you are simply going to wish me good-night, we could have done that in the passage."

He ignored this pleasant beginning. "I'm sure you are aware how dangerous your behavior was tonight."

Well. Nothing like jumping right in with both feet. "Certainly not. I had a good idea and attributed it to you, just as a self-sacrificing, supportive fiancée should."

"Sarcasm is an unbecoming trait in a woman."

"As is deceit in a man."

"I am deceiving no one. As I explained to you before, we are just being careful about the timing of the information we give. To everything there is a season."

"And it is my season to be cast in your shadow?"

He gazed at her as she perched bolt upright on the chair opposite him. "I had not suspected this need for recognition in you, this constant desire to be in the spotlight. It is unwomanly."

"I desire no such thing, except to receive credit where it is due. You are baldly taking credit for my ideas and hard work, and it is becoming increasingly hard to bear. How I shall get through the next couple of days in Mr. Stephenson's company without telling him the truth, I do not know."

"Then perhaps you should retire to your cottage by the river and look after your charges."

Her temper was rolling at a fine boil by now. "Perhaps I should do so on a permanent basis."

"What do you mean?"

"I cannot live like this, James."

"Like what? In modesty, content to allow men of business to conduct their business?"

"It is *my* business as well. Andrew treats me as an equal. He would never dream of passing off my ideas as his own, temporarily or not."

"Ah, Andrew. And do you view him as such a paragon, and me a villain?"

"I base my views on observation, as any good scientist would do."

"But you are not a scientist."

"Perhaps not yet by education, but certainly by inclination."

"And do you see your current behavior as promoting those ends?" For a moment she was silenced, and he followed up on his advantage. "I have not made up my mind yet about whether to do as your mother asks and insist on an autumn wedding, or to allow you to attend university."

Her jaw tightened at *insist* and *allow*, words he wielded as carelessly as he wielded power over her.

"I have noticed that," she said with forced calm. "Particularly in your mention of the letters of recommendation. But I do not need Mr. Stephenson's letter. Not if we exhibit the device and my name is on the patent."

"The name of a willful, self-aggrandizing woman will not go on that patent."

HER OWN DEVICES

She stared at him, fingers twisting in the satin folds of the bottle-green dinner gown she had borrowed from her mother, as her blood slowed in its course and froze with horror. "What did you say?"

"I am completely willing to put the name of a cooperative, supportive woman on that patent and acknowledge her help in creating the device. I am not so willing to do so for someone who will not do as I ask, who is short-sighted and selfish, and who puts her own needs before those of others and endangers a business venture that has been in the making for two long years."

It took at least ten seconds before Claire could master herself and not fly at him the way the Mopsies would, fingernails first.

"Are you blackmailing me?" she whispered through stiff lips.

"Certainly not. Simply presenting the terms of an agreement."

She must break off their engagement. She must rid herself of this man as soon as possible before she committed an act of which society would most certainly not approve. Her trigger finger twitched, and she wound her fingers together.

But if she jilted him, he would certainly expunge her name from the patent, from the exhibit, from the application that would gain her what she so dearly wanted.

Just another few days.

Once her name was published on that patent, she would throw him over so hard his posterior would never recover.

"As you wish," she finally said.

"You will abide by my terms and stop endangering this deal with your behavior?"

"Yes."

He let out a long breath. "I am glad." Rising, he took her cold hand and helped her to her feet. "Thank you. I realize my methods have dampened your spirits somewhat, but in the long run you will not regret it."

She did not answer, simply preceded him to the door of her room.

"You look very nice tonight, Claire. May I say that that color suits you admirably."

The door closed in his face.

HER OWN DEVICES

21

"Lady," Tigg said as the gentlemen left the salon car and went forward to talk to the engineer on the long, flat run before the grade into London, "I fink the Mopsies are right."

Claire felt fit to burst out of her corset. "About what, Tigg?" She leapt to her feet and began to pace from one end of the car to the other. Ten down, ten back, her traveling skirts swishing like the tail of an angry cat.

"About 'is ni—er, 'is lordship. Beggin' yer pardon, but they don't like 'im."

"I know. At the moment, I don't like him very much, either."

"'E's leavin' you behind in this venture. But what I

SHELLEY ADINA

don't get is why you or at least Mr. Malvern don't fix it."

"I don't believe Mr. Malvern is aware of it. Or if he is, he believes I am going along with it and will not speak up out of delicacy."

"Why *are* you goin' along wiv it, Lady?"

There was the crux of the matter. "I want my name on that patent, Tigg. I must play my part in this charade until that happens."

"And then what? You give 'is nibs the air?"

Not for worlds would she reveal her inmost thoughts. Not that Tigg would talk, but it was not easy to look at herself and realize that she had let herself in for the whole thing. If she had not been swayed by the idiotic thought of being the first of her set to be engaged, of being the one sought after for a change instead of pitied, then she would not be in such an awkward, uncomfortable, maddening position now.

She had lost sight of herself in the vision of how others saw her, and now she had to pay the price.

"A lady does not give anyone the air, Tigg. She acknowledges the honor of his proposal and declines it with grace."

"But you're going to, aye? Decline with grace? Coz I'll say this, I don't think 'is lordship is going to take kindly to our continued association, if you get my meaning."

"I made a promise to you all, and I shall keep it."

"'Ow? Wot if 'e turns us all out?"

"He will not."

"If yer 'is wife, Lady, you'll 'ave to do as 'e says.

And if 'e says to turf the lot of us, then there ent much you could do to stop it."

"It will not come to that, Tigg."

But perhaps it would. If she felt oppressed and imprisoned as his fiancée, how would she manage when she was his wife, and all her worldly goods belonged to him, including her very person?

Girls from families like hers had been born and bred for such an eventuality. But girls from families like hers did not end up as leaders of South Bank gangs. And once one had had a taste of respect and authority, it was downright difficult to give it up.

"No, it shall not come to that," she murmured. She hadn't meant for Tigg to hear, but his ears were sharp. He sat back and concentrated on the view rushing past the window at fifty miles per hour, and said no more.

When they reached London, nothing would do but that Mr. Stephenson should go immediately to the laboratory. Claire had thought he might go to an hotel, or at the very least, to James's club, but no-ho. His impatience to see the chamber in action brought them all to Orpington Close in a hansom cab.

Since she was not permitted to be of use, like Tigg, she repaired to the office above to wait until they were finished. She stripped off her gloves and laid her hat on the desk, then walked over to check the mail repository.

Several tubes lay within. One after the other, she sorted them—invoices, a note from Andrew's mother reminding him of a family birthday party, a letter from the Royal Society giving particulars of the submission process for the new exhibit.

That she read with interest, making mental notes on which points she might best assist.

The last tube contained a piece of hotel stationery, and had been forwarded from Greenwich, whence came all the international mail into the country.

Dear Claire,

Our voyage over the Atlantic was every bit as exciting and interesting as you could imagine. There are fifty passengers, plus the crew, and though accommodations are rather tight, what could be lovelier than waking to a view of nothing but sky of a morning? I'm half tempted to sign up as crew myself, though what I would do is a mystery. There are no decks to swab; however, I could do a passable job at polishing brass, of which there is an abundance.

But enough of my nonsense.

I am bidden to convey the greetings of a friend of yours—Dr. Rosemary Craig, who sails with us. She and my mother have become great cronies, and in fact, since her plans were quite nebulous—oh, to be so free that you could take ship for nowhere in particular!—we have invited her to come along to the Canadas with our party. San Francisco will be there whenever she gets to it, but an adventure in the diamond mines with my esteemed mother is not to be missed.

If you are of a mind to write to her, you may use our address at the hotel in Edmonton. Such fun!

I trust you are well and happy. I am still waiting

for the end of that sentence. I find myself fascinated by all the possibilities.

New York is calling. I do wish you were here—we could have made this town our own.

Warmly, I remain
Your friend Peony Churchill

Claire folded up the letter and tucked it in her reticule. What a relief to know that Dr. Craig had made a clean escape—and whether or not Isabel Churchill knew of her history, her future as a crony of that lady was certain to be spectacular.

At the conclusion of the day she declined to have dinner with James, Andrew, and Mr. Stephenson, and declined as well the offer of the cab. In this, at least, she could exercise her independence.

She'd come to a pretty pass when taking the Underground was an act of rebellion. But in the doing of it, she firmed her resolve. She would not marry James under any circumstances, even if it meant going into hiding even deeper than she already was until her eighteenth birthday. She would see her name safely on that patent, secure the letter of recommendation from Andrew, and move on with her life as a university student and governess to the children.

Mentally, she waved farewell to Lady Selwyn, Baroness, that fictional being who had never had any more substance than smoke.

She had never really liked her anyway.

Andrew heard Claire and Tigg arrive the next day for their morning's work. When they saw that the laboratory was empty, they climbed the stairs to find him up to his elbows in paper from the Patent Office.

"Where are Lord James and Mr. Stephenson?" Tigg asked, tying his leather apron around his waist as if he expected to begin disassembly of the device that moment. "Didn't they say the chamber was to be packed up and ready to move?"

"They did, and it will be." Andrew picked up a sketch and numbered it. "They've gone to the Crystal Palace this morning to enter it as an exhibit. They're calling it the Selwyn Kinetick Carbonator. Once Ross Stephenson gets a bee in his bonnet, there's no stopping him. I can't see them turning him down, either. Between James's influence in Parliament and Ross's importance in industry, it's a given."

"And what about the patent?" Claire looked pale and a little drawn, as if she had not slept very well. But a gentleman would never let such an observation cross his lips.

Andrew indicated the pile of drawings and forms that covered the desk. "They left that to me. A patent application must sponsored by a member of the Royal Society of Engineers. At least in that I can be useful."

"I know what you mean," Claire said. She unwound a length of gauzy fabric from around her hat. "I have never felt more like a mantel scarf than I have this past few days. Entirely decorative, prone to gathering unwanted objects, and of no earthly use whatsoever."

He gazed at her, puzzled. "But James said you preferred the company of Lady Elizabeth. Something about missing adult female companionship."

"Bullfeathers," Claire snapped, surprising him with the barely contained force of the outburst. "The unpalatable truth is that Ross Stephenson believes women are mantel scarves. James would not allow me even to join your discussions, much less inform Mr. Stephenson that I had invented the movable truss."

Aghast, Andrew put the pen down, where it proceeded to ooze a blob of ink on a sketch of the control levers. "But that is criminal. Why did you not tell me?"

"Because 'is nibs said 'e wouldn't put 'er name on the patent if she didn't keep mum," Tigg said, gracelessly putting his oar into the conversational waters.

Claire rounded on him. "Tigg! That is a confidence between his lordship and me, and none of your business." She narrowed her gaze at him. "And how did you hear of it, pray?"

"The nursery is straight above that little room you were talkin' in, Lady. I can't help it if voices come up the stove pipe, clear as day, if you just open the stove door."

"Good heavens." She struggled for control—perhaps of her language, certainly of her temper. "You have succeeded in humiliating me in front of Mr. Malvern, Tigg. Thank you very much."

Tigg's face fell in lines of distress. "I didn't mean to, Lady," he said, his lower lip beginning to wobble. Perhaps, Andrew thought, she had never spoken to him sharply before—and she had not realized that her good opinion was so important to him that the loss of it would reduce him to tears. "I just wanted Mr. M-Malvern to 'ave the t-truth."

She crossed the room to take him in her arms, leather apron and all. "It's all right, Tigg," she said gently. "Of course you did, and it was honorable of you to want to set the record to rights. But you must remember that information gained by eavesdropping must be kept confidential. It can be too hurtful otherwise."

"Y-yes, Lady." He sniffled into her shoulder, and she fished her handkerchief out of her white voile sleeve. He blew his nose and mopped his face, and offered the scrap of cambric back to her.

"Keep it, dear." She turned back to Andrew. "Well, now that you have the truth, I—"

"I cannot believe this of James." He felt so dazed that he interrupted her without thinking. "To use the patent as the condition of your effacing yourself? That does not seem like him—or like a gentleman, for that matter."

"As you can see, I have a witness," Claire said dryly.

Now it was Andrew's turn to voice his distress. "I didn't mean I distrusted your word. I meant that I thought I knew him better than this. I mean to say, putting the business first is one thing, if we must stay on Ross Stephenson's good side. But to require such a thing of his own fiancée ..." Andrew gathered his wits with an effort. "Well. We can only do what we can do, and since I am the one filling out this application, Claire's name will go where it belongs. While I am doing that, Tigg, you are quite correct. You should start disassembling the chamber and get it ready to be hauled out to the Crystal Palace. I sent a tube to a packing company first thing this morning, so we should expect a delivery of crates and straw at any time."

"Yes, sir."

"I have laid out a rough schematic of which sections should be crated together. You will find it on the workbench."

"Yes, sir."

"Tigg?"

"Yes, sir?"

"I am including you on this application in an adjunct capacity. But I cannot very well put *Tigg* in all its expressive simplicity. What is your full name?"

Tigg's eyes and mouth formed a trio of Os. "My name, sir?" he said at last. "On the patent? For true?"

"Yes, for true. What should I write down?"

"I 'ardly know, sir. I 'aven't used it since I was a little shaver." Andrew waited. Then, with a gulp, Tigg finally said, "Tom Terwilliger, sir."

"That's quite a handle," Claire said with a perfectly straight face.

"None of me mates could manage it, so they shortened it up for everyday."

"Thank you, Tigg." Andrew wrote *Thomas Terwilliger* in the blank. "Two Ls?"

"Dunno, sir."

"You have two Ls now. Thank you. I shall be down to help you in just a moment."

"Yes, sir." The boy clattered down the stairs and, moments later, they heard the sounds of clanking metal and glass as he got to work.

The moment they were alone, Andrew laid down his pen and stood, coming round the desk. He was still reeling from the knowledge that his partner, nobly born and up until now as honorable as the day was long, could stoop to blackmailing the woman he was supposed to marry.

"Do not," Claire said, her voice tight, as she held up a hand to ward him off. "Do not speak of it. It is bad enough that you know."

"You should have told me."

"To what end? So that you could think me spineless sooner rather than later?"

"I don't think you're spineless. Quite the opposite. It is James who has shocked me. Claire, if a man can treat you so abominably, what else is he capable of? I mean to say, once one has stooped to blackmail, what comes next?"

She turned away. "That is an ugly word. We merely came to the terms of an agreement."

"Unacceptable terms, agreed to under duress, if your face is any indication."

"My face is my business," she said. "All that matters is my name on that patent, and your letter of recommendation."

"Speaking of that, it's right here. With all the racketing around the country, this is the first chance I've had to give it to you."

He pulled the two closely written pages out of the top drawer of the desk, the second one with his Society seal already affixed.

She read them, and color rose in her face. Her features softened, and if he had not been under her spell before, he certainly would have fallen head over heels now. It was all he could do not to pull James's intended wife into his arms.

Surely she would not go through with the engagement, once the patent was secured? Surely she could not face life at the side of a man who would treat her as less than she was?

She looked up, her gray eyes swimming with tears she was too proud to shed. "Thank you," she said hoarsely. "I had not expected—that is, you are much too generous—"

"I hardly touched on the half," he said gently. "The university here should be glad you are even considering them, when you could go to Edinburgh or the Sorbonne and have them welcome you with open arms."

He realized a moment too late that he had illustrated his point with his own open arms. His body had gone where his mind had forbidden it, and now he looked like an utter fool.

He cleared his throat and got himself safely back in his chair again, the width and bulk of the desk between them. "You will be a great success, Claire," he said, striving for a hearty, brotherly tone. "Lady Selwyn will be the most brilliant woman in London."

"I'm sure she will," she said, and turned away to go down the steps.

It wasn't until he went to number another sketch that he realized how distant the words had sounded.

As if she hadn't meant herself at all.

22

The grand opening of the new exhibit wing at the Crystal Palace was the social event of the Wit season. Even the Bloods, whose tolerance of new technologies extended only to securing the newest versions of the mother's helper when they came out, could not stay away. Every newspaper in England seemed to be represented, and the *Times* of New York had sent a reporter over by airship so there would be no time lost between the unveiling of a new engine and its subsequent reproduction overseas.

The evening before the opening day, when the general public were to be admitted, a reception and ball were held under the sparkling glass panes of the exhibit hall. Between the huge iron support pillars and the potted palms, tables of food and refreshment had been set up, and down at one end, an orchestra tuned up its instruments. Everyone Claire greeted seemed to be in a tizzy of excitement.

"The Prince of Wales is expected, you know," someone told his partner immediately behind Claire. Since he had been expected at the Wellesley's fancy-dress ball and had not come, Claire did not put much stock in this.

She was, however, presented to His Royal Highness Prince Albert, who was representing Her Majesty, and whose particular project was the entire Crystal Palace itself.

"Your Royal Highness," James said, "may I present my fiancée, Lady Claire Trevelyan."

She dipped into her lowest curtsey, thankful that the poker players had had a particularly good week and she had been able to buy a new gown for the occasion. A deep sapphire blue, it had the barest suggestion of cap sleeves and was pleated tightly in a vee on the bodice that arrowed down to a tiny waist, with a satisfying long train faced in black velvet trailing out behind. The Mopsies had pounced on a pair of kid opera gloves at Portobello Road, with only a tiny stain on the palm of the left one, and to her astonishment, James had presented her with a diamond necklace when she had climbed into his coach at the laboratory.

"To celebrate your triumph," he had said simply. "It was my mother's, and now it is yours."

To remind you of our agreement, she heard. *You will act like a Blood and not a Wit.*

"It is a pleasure to meet you, my dear," the prince

said. "Please accept my belated condolences on the passing of your father, the viscount."

"You are very kind, Sir," she said. "I know he held you in the highest esteem for your support of England's position at the forefront of industry. Sir, may I present Mr. Thomas Terwilliger?" She clutched Tigg by the back of his brand-new morning coat before he could dodge behind the chamber. "He is Mr. Malvern's laboratory assistant and was instrumental in the initial construction and subsequent redesigns of the Selwyn Kinetick Carbonator."

His face as pale as his coffee-colored skin would allow, his eyes enormous, Tigg bobbed a bow. "Sir," he whispered.

"This young boy?" His Highness said in some astonishment. "Helped to construct this chamber? Why, he can't be more than thirteen."

"He did, Sir." Andrew stepped away from the control console and gripped Tigg's shoulder as if to say, *Courage, man.* "I predict a bright future in engineering for him."

The Prince gazed down at him, and Claire feared that Tigg might actually faint under the royal regard. "Young man, when it comes time to apply for university, I hope you will send me a note. It is my honor to be patron of the Royal Society of Engineers, you know, and if what Andrew says is true, I would be pleased to provide a letter of recommendation for you."

"For me?" Tigg gulped. "You'd do better to give the Lady one, Sir. It were she wot invented the movable truss."

The prince blinked, and before anyone could say another word, Lord James moved in, smiling and guiding His Highness around to the other side of the chamber, where Claire heard him say that there would be a demonstration of the chamber's power in less than an hour.

"Bravely done, Tigg," she murmured, pretending to adjust the lie of his coat. "Ineffective, but very bravely done, and I thank you for it."

"'E were only funnin' me, weren't he, Lady? He didn't really mean it about the letter."

Lord James, it would seem, had tainted more than one person's faith in the promises of others.

"On the contrary. Prince Albert's word is as good as a gold guinea. If he instructed you to send a note, then depend upon it, he will write a journal entry to that effect. His memory is prodigious—and his journals are even more so."

"Cor," Tigg breathed. "Who'd 'ave thought?"

"Tigg," Andrew said, coming around the side of the chamber, "I require your assistance if we are to make the demonstration on time."

Claire stood back, watching them load coal into the chamber and secure the cowling and pipes. They had modified the design so that the entire engine would be relatively portable, making it more attractive to the railroad men, who would not have to build new edifices to house it. It also meant that, unlike some of the engines in the exhibit, which had to depend on schematics to explain their workings, theirs could be demonstrated on the spot, to spectacular effect.

"Lady Claire Trevelyan?"

Claire turned to see a man in white tie at her elbow. "Yes?"

"His Royal Highness Prince Albert requests the honor of the first waltz, milady, to open the dancing at ten o'clock."

She devoutly hoped her astonishment did not show on her face. By order of precedence that honor should go to the most senior lady present, which in this case was the Duchess of Devonshire, holding court over there by the champagne punch.

"I am Percival Mount-Batting, personal secretary to His Royal Highness," the man went on. "What answer may I convey to him?"

Ah. One of Robert's cousins, said to be in line for a baronetcy for his service to the Crown. He must be a very good secretary indeed.

"Please offer him my thanks and tell him I would be deeply honored," she said.

Dear oh dear. Perhaps he would not notice the spot on her left glove. Perhaps the entire female contingent at the ball would not notice, either.

But she would be noticed. It would be in the papers tomorrow that she had danced with the Prince Consort. Goodness, how Julia and Catherine and the rest would fume!

No, no. That kind of thinking had got her so deeply in trouble that it was all she could do to stay afloat. She must leave off thinking like a schoolgirl.

What would she talk about with a prince as they waltzed among the sparkling pillars and under the fronds of the palms? She had no talent for small talk, and no personal details she was prepared to divulge.

Engineering, of course. That was it. Had he not just said he was the patron of the Royal Society? What a relief!

If it had been the Prince of Wales she would have to go and seek out the smelling salts. He was such a randy-dandy that no woman of virtue was said to be safe with him. This was probably why he was so madly popular among the titled set, and why nabbing him for her guest list was every hostess's dream.

While she had stood there woolgathering, Andrew and Tigg had prepared the chamber, and a crowd had gathered.

"Please stand back," James advised them. "And shield your eyes—the power of this device can blind you for several seconds."

He gave an introductory speech, which mentioned neither Claire's part in the development of the chamber nor the impending deal with the Midlands Railroad Company. They must have appropriated her idea and were waiting for its fame to go far and wide before they made the announcement, in order to get the most publicity.

At last it was time.

Andrew activated the chamber and the movable truss. The familiar hum sounded even over the buzz of conversation and the clink of glasses. When it reached its operating pitch, Andrew raised an arm, then lowered it sharply. Tigg shoved the levers up and a flash of light caused men to gasp and ladies to cry out.

When the smoke cleared from the chamber, everyone

surged forward to look, while James explained the coal's new properties and what it could accomplish. Claire moved back against a pillar, cradling her glass of punch, and realized a moment too late that she had put herself in the company of Ross Stephenson.

He smiled at her as if she had done it on purpose. "A grand sight, eh?" He, too, was dressed in white tie, which only succeeded in making his face look more florid. "We shall be the talk of the town."

"I was surprised that James did not mention your joint venture in his remarks," Claire said. "Are you waiting for a more opportune time for the announcement?"

"We're waiting for the blasted solicitors to draw up the contracts. Lawyers. Have no-ho idea of the importance of timing." He gulped his champagne punch as if it were water.

"That may be all to the good, though," she said. "Let the anticipation, the newspaper reports, the public approbation build to a fever pitch, and then make the announcement. That will keep the Midlands Railroad uppermost in the public mind."

He laughed and patted her shoulder. "You've been talking with James, I see."

"No, I—"

"He's a good man. Sharp. I like a man who gathers good minds around him. Like that Malvern fellow. Sharp."

"Like myself and Tigg, as well," came out of her mouth before her brain could engage and stop the words.

"Eh? Yes, of course. A good wife is—"

Again the rush of words, spilling out of her with no semblance of control. "I am not his wife yet. And I must correct a slight misunderstanding, since you will see the patent when it is assigned ... I am the inventor of that movable truss, which creates the motion necessary to build up the kinetick charge."

"Eh?" His mouth hung open a little, making him look rather like some of the unfortunates in Bedlam. "What's that you say?"

"We must all move with the times, Mr. Stephenson." She smiled at him. "A woman possessed of a fine intellect is as capable of contributing to the forward march of progress as any man."

"You—are you saying that you—a mere girl—? Impossible."

"Quite possible. Quite real. And quite a success, as you can see." The crowd had begun to disperse, chattering among themselves about the breakthrough and all its possibilities.

"But James—"

"James concealed my involvement out of respect for your views and feelings, sir. But on this happy night, I only felt it proper that you should know the truth. And one more thing, while we're on the subject—that power cell on which your whole enterprise depends was invented by a woman. Doctor Rosemary Craig. You may have heard of her."

She gave him another brilliant smile and observed that now she had rendered him incapable of any speech at all. Trailing satin, velvet, and triumph, she walked away to inspect the buffet.

She had no doubt that he would hustle over to James and demand the truth as soon as he could speak. Well, James could just deal with it. She was tired of being shunted into the shadows and demeaned and patronized, and tonight at least, James could do nothing about it. If he so much as looked at her sideways, all of London would take note, and the gossip would be fearsome.

At five minutes to ten, she was still managing to elude him—not so difficult, since he had spent the last half hour engulfed in a loud crowd of what appeared to be Texicans, if their boots were any indication. The orchestra began tuning up in earnest.

But the one man whose job it was not to be eluded appeared at her elbow. Did he track down all the prince's partners and line them up like forks at a place setting?

"The opening waltz will begin shortly, milady," Percival Mount-Batting murmured. "If you will come with me?"

The orchestra played a chord and Prince Albert stepped up to a sound-amplifying horn mounted on a dais flanked by banked flowers.

"It is my great pleasure to declare the New Sciences Exhibit officially open. Please enjoy yourselves this evening, and marvel with me at the wonder of human endeavor."

The orchestra struck up the Treasure Waltz, and Claire slipped a wrist through the loop that lifted her train into dancing position, curtseyed, and stepped into the prince's arms. His hand was firm at her waist, his other hand lightly grasping hers. He was an exceedingly good dancer, guiding her about the expanse of the arcade as lightly as a fencing master. After the first turn, other dancers swirled into the pattern, and it was safe to converse.

"I am sorry Her Majesty was not able to accompany you, Sir," she said. "I understand she enjoys dancing."

"She does, indeed, but she is meeting with a delegation from India this evening. Some appallingly boring dinner which she is much better at managing than I am." Claire could not quite stifle a smile, and he saw it. "This is a treat for me, spending an evening in the company of minds with which I feel a kinship."

"I am happy to be part of it," she said.

"I understand you have a greater part in certain things than I had been led to believe. That young man said you invented the moving truss. Is that true, Lady Claire?"

"Yes, sir."

"Admirable. Her Majesty must hear of this. So then I must ask, why is your name not in the exhibit description?"

"It does not matter to me, Sir. What matters is that my name is on the patent application."

He was silent a moment, twirling her out and back in again in a figure of the waltz. "There is some skullduggery afoot here."

"No, merely a reluctance to crush a partner's illusions about the capabilities of women."

The prince made a most unprincely sound. "This

partner does realize that the greatest empire in the history of humankind is ruled by a woman?"

"It is a puzzle to me also, Sir."

"I will have this situation corrected if you wish it."

"No, Sir, though I thank you for your concern. In the larger scheme of things, the patent will last longer than people's memories of this evening."

"An unusual view for one so young."

"Youth does not preclude knowledge of people."

"In that you are correct. My dear wife could attest to it as well. I see that Percy is signaling us from the sidelines, so I am afraid that our partnership is at an end."

He whirled her back to the dais, where the Duchess of Devonshire raised her lorgnette to see who on earth had upstaged her.

"Thank you, Sir," Claire said. "For your kindness. And your powers of observation."

"I was an engineer before I was the consort of a queen." He bowed, and she curtseyed, once to him, and once to the Duchess, who lifted her chin and passed her with a nod stiff with frost.

Claire repaired to the punch bowl, her heart beating fast, both with relief that she had not tripped and embarrassed him, and exhilaration that at least two people outside the walls of the laboratory knew the truth. She had no doubt that enlightening Ross Stephenson would cause trouble of some kind, but the knowledge that the Prince Consort both knew and approved would bear her up during times of trial.

For she had spoken the truth to him—it was not the

public approbation she wanted. James could have his champagne and his crowds. She wanted a career, and it would begin with that patent.

James found her at the dessert table, savoring a fluffy little bite composed of candied fruit and sheer fancy. "Have you had your supper, dear?"

She had not much experience at galas of this kind, but even she knew a gentleman would have seen that she had all she needed long ago if he had not been wooing his cronies in the crowd.

"Yes, thank you. Try one of these, James. They are wonderful."

He accepted it and popped it in his mouth. "May I have the next?" She picked up another comfit but he shook his head. "I meant the next dance. It is a polka."

She ate the comfit herself. "Certainly."

He drifted off into the crowd again and she decided to join Andrew and Tigg at the chamber. Tigg saw her coming and pulled her off to the side.

"'Is nibs is in a fine fury," he said, stretching up so she could hear him. "If I was you, Lady, I'd stand 'im by the brandy and keep it coming."

He had not looked in a fury a moment ago. "Has something happened, Tigg? Did something go wrong with the chamber after the demonstration?"

Tigg ducked his head without answering and vanished around the control console as James approached and offered her his arm. "Shall we?"

Whatever he was angry about, he concealed it as they merged into the circle and the contagious beat that was all the rage in every capital of Europe took their feet under its spell. But halfway around the third circuit, James changed course and danced her out the end of the gallery into a courtyard garden arranged between the wings. "It is time for a little privacy with my intended," he said.

She could not see his face in the dark, so strolled in a short circle, pretending to admire their surroundings, until he was facing the brilliant lights of the exhibit hall. Still, his eyes were dark wells, and some emotion she could not identify sparked there.

"I hope you enjoyed your waltz with the prince."

"I did indeed, thank you. He is a very skilled dancer. And an interesting man of conversation."

"It is conversation that interests me, dear, now that you mention it. What the devil are you playing at, to announce your involvement in this project so clumsily to Ross Stephenson?"

He sounded almost casual. If it had not been for his language and the crispness of his consonants, she would not know he was angry. "It was time he knew the truth."

"And you are the one who decides the timing?"

"When it concerns me, yes."

"It concerns more than merely yourself. I was prepared to live with your self-centeredness, Claire, but bullheaded foolishness is quite another matter. It must stop."

Self-centered! Bullheaded! These were fine names to call someone who was merely trying to stand up for herself. "I am sorry my behavior distresses you. But I cannot unsay words that have been said."

"You may not, but I already have. I told him that you overstepped your bounds and were merely a secretary. That you had twisted filing the designs in your head with actually developing them."

"You what?" Claire whispered, so shocked that she was barely able to speak. "You told him I lied?"

"You put me in this position. Thank heaven I had already blacked out your name on the patent application, or he would have been more confused than he already is."

She stared. This second shock rendered her completely mute.

"Yes. I removed your name from the application." Gently, he held her bare upper arms in his warm hands. "It's only a temporary measure, so that Ross isn't offended. He put down a thousand pounds as earnest money this evening, when we were having drinks in Hanover Square and I showed him the application. It was a necessary measure. But don't be alarmed—the patent process takes a few months and we can add a name back in at any time. In fact," he said, drawing her closer, "it would be the perfect wedding gift. I could not think of anything more fitting for my bride."

First it had been only until they signed the contract. Now it was only until they signed the wedding license. What would be next? Only until they signed the parish register upon the birth of his heir?

Every woman has a threshold beyond which she will not go. And at this moment, Claire realized she had reached hers.

"No," she said.

"No?"

"No wedding gift. You will put my name back on that application, James, or there will be no wedding."

"Come now, dear. You can't tell me that a piece of paper is of more value than our union."

"I will tell you what is of value. My integrity. My self-respect. And my happiness. All of which you have battered down, leaving no walls within which to shelter a union."

"I think your emotions and offended pride have caused you to exaggerate."

"If anything, I am being remarkably civil, since at this moment my actual desire is for a vial of gaseous capsaicin."

"How very improbable. Not to mention unladylike."

"How fortunate that I have released you from our engagement, then."

"I'm afraid you cannot. If you recollect, you are under your mother's control until October. She and I have agreed on a wedding date, in fact. October fifteenth. The day before your birthday."

"Agree on as many days as you like. You will have to find me first."

With that, she snatched up her train and left him, her dancing slippers flying. Weaving through the crush, dodging around tables of food, she spotted Tigg next to the chamber gazing longingly at someone's plate.

"Billy Bolt!" she whispered as she hurried past.

Without an instant's hesitation, he fell in behind her. Andrew looked up from his conversation, mystified. "Claire? Tigg? Where are you going?"

But even for him, she did not stop. If she did, James would find some way to catch up, to stall her, and she would never escape. With the instincts of rabbits bounding over tussock and bramble for their bolt-hole, they headed not for the main doors, but back toward the open French doors the waiters had been using. Tigg lifted food from tables and plates as he went, stuffing them in his mouth as if he knew he would not get another opportunity.

The muted roar of conversation and the strains of the next waltz faded behind them as they gained the lawn. "What's 'appened, Lady?" Tigg panted.

Ah, there it was. James's coach stood ready, his coachman lounging in his seat with a glass of ale. "You there!" she called. "Lord James would like you to take me back to Hanover Square. We are to have drinks shortly with some of the Society men and their wives."

"At once, milady."

She had never stolen a coach before.

It was much easier than she thought.

23

Claire directed the coachman to leave her, not on the square where anyone could see, but in the mews behind the house. "I must make quick arrangements with Mrs. Morven," she told him, and he did not question her. He merely handed her to the pavement, waited for Tigg to jump out, and rattled off down the street, heading back to the exhibition to collect his employer.

Mrs. Morven had heard the coach, and despite the late hour, met them in the kitchen, tugging her wrap closed at the waist. "Why, Lady Claire! I thought you were at the Crystal Palace with his lordship. Not that I'm not glad to see you, but what ...?"

James had stolen her reputation and her future from her. A thousand pounds would not be reparation enough. Nevertheless, there were still good uses for it.

"Mrs. Morven, I know that you are loyal to your employer, but I must beg your help."

"Of course, dear. And as for loyalty, I wouldn't worry your head about that. I was loyal to you and your lady mother for long years before this."

Something in her expression made Claire pause. "What do you mean?"

"I mean that at least a woman could earn her keep in the Trevelyan household. His lordship has not given the staff their wages since I came to work for him."

Claire stopped edging toward the stairs and gave the woman her full attention. "Why should he do that? He will have a mutiny on his hands."

"He's about to get one. He keeps telling us that once he closes this railroad deal, there will be ample money. Once he marries you, miss, we will have a new home at Wilton Crescent. Once the future arrives, in other words, everything will come up roses, but in the meantime, I've got to whip up fancy dinners out of nothing but brisket and potatoes and whatever I can scour at the end of a market day."

Suddenly Claire realized why James had insisted on marrying her, when any other man would have abandoned her penniless family and dim prospects long ago. Ross Stephenson was a man susceptible to the lure of a title. He had married a widow to get an entree into society for his children. He had formed a relationship with James, who came of an ancient family, and with her, whose parents had moved in the best circles, so that he could move in those circles, too. The earnest money he had so eagerly laid down before the contracts were signed proved it.

"Lord James has no money, either," she said, almost to herself. "He has been putting your wages into development of the chamber. If he doesn't sign the deal with Ross Stephenson, he will be ruined."

"I am afraid he is not the catch either of us imagined, miss."

"No. That is why I have broken my engagement."

"Have you, miss?" Mrs. Morven smiled. "I knew you had some sense, though your lady mother will disagree."

"Sense perhaps, but very little time. Would you mind if I ran upstairs to his lordship's study? Since we are no longer engaged, I cannot in good conscience wear these diamonds. I wish to return them to his desk, where they will be safe."

"Of course, miss. Young man, would you like a glass of milk while you wait?"

She devoutly hoped that James did not have a safe in his study. Perhaps in the bonhomie of having drinks with Stephenson, he would have put the money somewhere as a temporary measure until he got home. It was the work of a moment to rifle through his desk and find a cigar box, and sure enough, there were ten hundred-pound notes in it.

She had no intention of stealing his money for herself. But Andrew would lose everything once James's perfidy was discovered, as it surely would be now that he had misplaced his fiancée. She fetched a mailing tube and found a piece of the baronial crested stationery.

A—
For you.
J.

Hopefully Andrew would not realize the nearly illegible scrawl was not that of his partner until it was too late. She rolled nine of the bank notes into the tube, inserted the note, and the hydraulic system sucked it away into the night.

Then she unclasped the diamond necklace and laid it in the cigar box, replacing it exactly where she'd found it and erasing all signs of her presence.

Mrs. Morven nearly fainted when Claire presented her with the hundred-pound note. "You should divide this among the staff. Mrs. Morven, I am going away for several weeks. Thank you for everything you have done for me. I consider you a true friend."

With a quick hug and a kiss on that lady's hair, Claire hitched up her train once more, called to Tigg at the kitchen table, and the two of them vanished into the night.

TO: PEONY CHURCHILL
      CANADIAN PACIFIC HOTEL, EDMONTON
FROM: CLAIRE TREVELYAN, LONDON

AM COMING TO JOIN YOU STOP TAKING
PACKET TO PARIS THEN PERSEPHONE STOP

SHELLEY ADINA

EXPECT ME SECOND WEEK SEPTEMBER STOP JILTED JAMES STOP NEED HUG END

When Claire returned from the telegraph office, she was so focused on her list of items to be accomplished that it took her a moment to realize there was a gorgeous Bentley steam landau parked overlooking the river in the spot usually reserved for hers. She brought the Henley to a stop and initiated its cooling sequence, her hands moving automatically.

Who on earth ...?

The watchman on the river platform had her answer. "We gots company, Lady," he called down. "A lord and ladyship—Willie's mum and dad."

"The Dunsmuirs are here?" she exclaimed in amazement. "How on earth did they find us?"

This was catastrophic. She had counted on being invisible for the few days it would take her to wind up her affairs and board the *Princess Louise* for Paris. Of course she could have flown in *Persephone* from Southampton, but an initial gambit to throw James off her trail should he make inquiries was worth the day or two delay to her real journey.

She had not informed the children yet.

And was not looking forward to having to do so.

The watchman laughed. "Willie, o' course, Lady. 'E knows 'is way home as well as any of us."

Of course. Relief swept through her. She would just have to swear Lord and Lady Dunsmuir to secrecy on the subject, that was all.

She found the couple in the garden, watching Willie's delight in seeing the chickens again. "Hello, Lady Claire." Lord Dunsmuir shook hands, but Lady Dunsmuir clasped her in a hug that told Claire she was gaining her strength back in leaps and bounds now that she had her beloved son home again. "We've just been admiring your walking coop," his lordship went on. "Miss Lizzie says that Doctor Rosemary Craig assisted them in its construction. Most singular."

"A story for a long evening," Claire said with a smile. "But suffice to say that Doctor Craig is perfectly sane and healthy, and she is at present enjoying her travels out of the country."

Rosie marched up and tugged upon her skirt, demanding her attention, and Claire picked her up. The hen cuddled into her arms with the air of a queen resting upon her jeweled cushions, and surveyed her kingdom from on high.

"Most singular," Lord Dunsmuir murmured.

Two of the boys brought the table out into the sunshine, and Granny Protheroe proceeded to lay out tea.

"Where've you been, Lady?" Lizzie wanted to know.

"You didn't go to the laboratory?" Tigg asked. "If 'is nibs were there you might be in danger."

Lady Dunsmuir's eyebrows rose, and Claire hastened to explain as she took a seat. "I did not go to the laboratory. I have been visiting Mr. Arundel and sending telegrams." She gazed at them all—Snouts, Jake, the Mopsies, Lewis, Tigg, and the others—and her heart broke at having to leave them. But it had to be done. "Has Tigg told you that I have broken my engagement to Lord James?"

The Mopsies nodded. "And good riddance, too."

Lady Dunsmuir made a sound suspiciously like a laugh, picked up the teapot, and began to pour for all of them, her face appropriately sober once more.

"He is not ... taking it well. I am very much afraid he will force me to marry him before my eighteenth birthday, so I am going on a trip." They stirred, and looked at each other with a mixture of excitement and trepidation. "I am going to visit Miss Churchill and Doctor Craig in the Canadas. I shall return in six weeks, after my birthday, so I'll be back before you know it."

Maggie sidled up to her and stroked Rosie's feathers, and Willie came to her other side, laying his little hand upon her knee. "But what about us, Lady? Are we to go, too?"

"I—I am afraid not. I have cashed out my stock in the Midlands Railroad—" *And put half of it in shares of Count Zeppelin's airships.* "—but even then, I could only afford passage for one."

"Not go?" Maggie's eyes filled. "But you promised. We're flock mates. We're always to be together. You said so."

Oh, dear. "I know, but it's only for—"

"You *said* so! You *promised!*" Maggie burst into tears, and Lizzie followed suit, and then Willie, too.

Claire felt her own eyes fill, and before she knew it, all the strain and emotional upheaval of the past few days overwhelmed her, and her breath hitched in a sob. "I'm sorry," she choked out. "I must go where he cannot reach me—I don't know what else—"

Lady Dunsmuir telegraphed an urgent message to

her husband with her fine, expressive eyes.

"Lady Claire, if I might offer a suggestion?"

He could hardly be heard above the wailing. Rosie, disturbed by the noise and kerfuffle, jumped down from Claire's lap and stalked away into the pea arbor, where she vented her displeasure on the unfortunate rooster.

Claire controlled herself with difficulty, swiping her wet cheeks with the palm of her hand. "Yes, m-my lord?"

"It seems to be the season to make travel plans. Since Willie returned to us, Davina and I have been vexed to the point of near violence by newspaper reporters camped outside the door, and sundry evil gossips making free with our names in public. We have decided to take an extended tour of my family's holdings and enterprises in the Canadas until the furor dies down. We are, in fact, leaving tomorrow. This is why we came to visit—Willie would not rest until he had said goodbye to each and every one of his friends, including that extraordinary hen."

Claire slipped an arm around Willie's shoulders and kissed the top of his head. "You darling, always thinking of others before yourself." She sniffled. "We should have been dreadfully upset to have come to call, only to find you all gone."

"Claire, would you consider accompanying us?" Lady Dunsmuir's soft voice silenced the crying, and the girls subsided into sniffles themselves. Claire pulled her handkerchief out of her sleeve and handed it to Maggie. "And the children, too, as many as wish to go, so that you will not be separated, and Willie will have companions with whom to enjoy the adventure?"

Claire's breath went out of her in a rush. "My goodness, how kind you are—but we could not—the expense!"

Lord Dunsmuir waved a negligent hand. "Oh, we do not travel on *Persephone*. *Lady Lucy*, the family airship named for my grandmother, is moored at Southampton. Between my father, rest his soul, and my younger brothers, one of us has always been in the air either coming or going from our business in the Canadas. Believe me, there is room for you and your household, as our most honored guests."

A private airship—! Goodness, the Dunsmuirs must be wealthier than she had ever dreamed.

"We are staying at the hotel at Waterloo Station, and will take the seven o'clock train to Southampton tomorrow morning."

And to travel in the comfort and companionship of a family she had learned to respect ... suddenly the prospect of traveling alone to the other side of the world held no appeal whatsoever. "I should love to share the adventure with you," she said. "And the children—you are sure—?"

"If they agree to come, I can have a word at the Home Office and have traveling papers prepared within the hour. I assume you have yours."

She did, having secured them during her errands this morning. Goodness. Well. All that remained was to determine who would go. "Mopsies? What say you?"

"We're going," Maggie said promptly. "I like airships." Lizzie looked a little ill, but where her twin went, there she went also.

Willie grinned, left Claire's side, and went to hug his

mother, as if in thanks for arranging the entire enterprise.

"Tigg?"

"I—I dunno, Lady. I feel beholden to Mr. Malvern, but I want to stick wi' you. Then there's the landau to be thought of."

"You have a steam landau?" his lordship asked. "Even better. Ours goes with us on the cargo deck. Yours will balance the load. It is simply a matter of driving them up into a boxcar and tying down the wheels."

For every problem, he provided a solution. How lucky Lady Davina was to have a man who lived positively instead of negatively.

"If the landau and the Lady go, then I go," Tigg said, lifting his chin as if to challenge anyone who disputed it. "I s'pose Mr. Malvern will understand, since our project is done with and I dunno what he'll be working on next."

"Snouts?" Claire asked. "Jake? Lewis?"

Lewis shook his head. "No airships for me, nor Rosie either. I'll stay and look after the chickens."

"Nor me," Snouts told her. "Beggin' yer pardon, Lady, but I'm better off on t'ground where I know what's what. Someone 'as to be in charge of this lot, and it won't be you, Lewis."

Jake mumbled something, and at Claire's prodding, said, "'Er ladyship did give me yer uncle's coat. Shame to waste it."

"It would be. I should appreciate your companionship and protection, Jake, if you would come."

He glanced up under his shaggy hair at the Earl of Dunsmuir. "If 'is lordship don't mind?"

"Certainly not," he said stoutly. "I should be glad of a man's company. And it doesn't hurt to learn a thing or two about aerial navigation. Captain Hollys is a fine teacher, despite the fact that it's taken years to pound such facts into my thick skull."

Lady Dunsmuir clapped her hands like a delighted child. "Then we are agreed. We shall share this adventure together. In fact, if you can gather your things on such short notice, we can leave now and spend the night in the hotel. I understand they serve a particularly fine roast beef and Yorkshire pudding."

And so it was decided, with less fanfare than it took to plan a dinner party.

Claire required only moments to pack the clothes for herself and the girls, along with enough notebooks to record their journey—the only difficulty being where to conceal the lightning rifle, for she would not leave it behind. Finally she rolled it up in her driving duster and strapped it to the outside of her traveling case, which was stuffed with the extra burden of the blue satin ballgown and her leather corselet, driving goggles, and riding hat.

She would not leave her raiding rig behind, either, or a small supply of gaseous capsaicin and enough small parts and gears to construct a firelamp or two.

Because it was a big world out there, and one just never knew.

A lady of resources and intellect always faced the future prepared.

Epilogue

Dear Claire,

I am writing to you in shame and great distress. After you departed the Crystal Palace last night, the most appalling scandal broke out involving someone we both know well.

I hardly know how to say this, so I will just write it baldly: James has absconded with our chamber. Worse, he has sold it to a consortium of Texicans who promised to triple the deal that Ross Stephenson offered him. I say him because I have been completely cut out. All I have are the bolts on the exhibit floor that were left after they carted the entire chamber out in the small hours of the morning. From what I have been able to *discover, James and the Texicans plan to shoulder their way onto one of the transatlantic airships that accept heavy cargo, and flee before agents of the Midland Railroad Company catch them.*

For some reason that mystifies me, he has tried to make reparation by sending me money. I will use it to pursue them. Needless to say, it is my livelihood and reputation that are at stake.

I swear, Claire, that I will get the kinetick cell back. Dr. Craig said it was yours. It is one thing to use it to make our own living in an honorable way. It is quite another to steal the entire device and flee the country. But without the cell, the chamber will be nothing more than glass and brass, and we will see how clever the Texicans are at carbonating coal without it.

I do not know when I will see you again.

I hope you will think of me kindly.

Yours in haste,
Andrew Malvern

THE END

A NOTE FROM SHELLEY

Dear reader,

I hope you enjoy reading the adventures of Lady Claire and the gang in the Magnificent Devices world as much as I enjoy writing them. It is your support and enthusiasm that is like the steam in an airship's boiler, keeping the entire enterprise afloat and ready for the next adventure.

You might leave a review on your favorite retailer's site to tell others about the books. And you can find the electronic editions of the entire series online, as well as audiobooks. I'll see you over at www.shelleyadina.com, where you can sign up for my newsletter and be the first to know of new releases and special promotions.

And now, I invite you to turn the page for an excerpt from *Magnificent Devices*, the next book in the series …

SHELLEY ADINA

Excerpt

MAGNIFICENT DEVICES
BY SHELLEY ADINA
© 2012

1

Somewhere over the Atlantic
Late September 1889

The man's eyes bulged in his final moments and he glared with brutal accusation. "You—" he choked. "You did it … you'll regret it …"

She faltered back, but her feet tangled in her apple-green skirts and she couldn't run. Still he staggered toward her.

"You—" Those eyes, filling her vision. Hazel eyes under auburn hair. James's eyes in another man's face. And then they boiled over, sizzling like bacon on a griddle, and popped and she screamed—

—and woke herself up. The breath left her lungs and

Lady Claire Trevelyan flopped back on the bunk with a gasp. Sweat trickled down her temple.

Breathe. You must breathe.

Lightning Luke had met his Maker several weeks ago at her hands, and while he might have found some measure of peace, she had not. Most of the time she was able to tamp down the guilt at having ended the life of another human being. It had been an accident. But in the midnight hours, there was his face again, contorted and boiling and accusing her until his last breath.

It was always so real, even if she had never actually seen his eyes. Her mind had put those of another in that face, one she had wronged, as if he—

Something rustled in the dark.

Claire sucked in a breath. It was not Lightning Luke. He was in a watery grave, to the best of her knowledge. It was not even Lord James Selwyn, who was in London. She was safe aboard the Lady Lucy, the luxury airship belonging to John, Earl Dunsmuir, and his wife Davina, to whom she had restored Willie, their son, not a week past.

Her cabin, while comfortably appointed with a velvet coverlet on a bed set into a kind of curved cupboard, and gleaming paneling that set off the visiting chairs, was not large. She could cross it in six steps, and by now, the third night of their voyage, she knew its topography by heart.

"Maggie?" she whispered. Perhaps one of the Mopsies had awakened in the night and needed her. "Lizzie?"

A thump, followed by scratching that somehow communicated agitation. This time, she could pinpoint its location: above, in the brass piping that ran along the floors and ceilings conveying heat, gas, and various other necessities in an airship this size.

She reached for a moonglobe. That was what the countess called them, she being of a gentle and fanciful turn of mind. Claire had inquired of the chief steward what they were, and he had launched into such an enthusiastic explanation of its properties ("One cannot have lamps and flames on an airship, my lady—only think of the gas fuselage above our heads!") that even she had been astonished that so much clever chemistry could be cupped in her hand. She shook the globe and it lit from within as the chemicals combined, illuminating the entire room.

No one was there.

But something was. Something that scratched, and clinked, and—was that a flutter? Good heavens, did bats lodge in the high ceilings of the passenger deck?

She lifted the globe and peered upward, and an enormous winged shadow leaped down upon her head.

She choked down a second scream that wanted to rattle the pipes, and grabbed for the shadow. It fought back, a limbless fighting ball of claws and feathers that—

Feathers?

Claire pounced on the moonglobe she'd dropped and held it up.

The fighting claws and feathers landed on the nightstand and resolved themselves into a small red hen, who shook her plumage into order and glared at her with offended dignity.

"Rosie?" Claire's knees gave out and she sat in the opening to her bunk rather suddenly. This couldn't be Rosie, the alpha hen of the flock of rescued chickens at the cottage in Vauxhall. The Dunsmuirs must have a small flock aboard for eggs, though with the powers of modern refrigeration, this seemed rather bucolic and unnecessary.

The hen stepped daintily off the nightstand and onto her knee, settling there as if she meant to spend the night.

She always did this. And it never worked.

"Rosie, for goodness sake. How on earth did you come to be on the Lady Lucy when I thought you were safe at home?" She petted the hen, speaking softly. "Lewis is going to be frantic, to say nothing of your flock. You will be supplanted by that rooster, my girl, and there will be no going back."

The door cracked open and in the greenish-white light of the moonglobe, Claire could see a two-inch-wide sliver of white batiste nightie. "Come in, Maggie."

"I 'eard a noise, Lady. All right?"

"Yes, quite all right. Come and see who has taken ship with us."

If she had expected Maggie to fall on Rosie's neck rejoicing, she was sadly disappointed. She looked almost ... guilty. "Hullo, Rosie." She stroked the gleaming feathers with gentle fingers, and Claire put two and two together.

"Maggie, did you know Rosie had stowed away?"

Maggie chewed on her lower lip. "She ent no trouble, Lady. She's bunked wiv us before."

"True on both counts. But that does not answer my question."

The ten-year-old's eyes filled with pleading. "She wanted to come, Lady. So I tucked 'er in my kit and she were quiet as the grave … 'til she found out she could roost up there." When she lifted her eyes to the pipes, a tear escaped down her cheek. "She's been up in the pipes a day and a half and I couldn't get 'er down."

"She'll be hungry, then."

"Aye. And thirsty."

"Then we will nip along to the dining saloon. You know Mr. Skully keeps a cold collation on the sideboard in case the family wishes a snack in the night."

"I know. Me and Lizzie, we found Willie an' Tigg in there two nights in a row. Willie can't keep out of the trifle. Nor can Lizzie, except when she's underfoot in the guardsroom and the gondola."

The little monkeys. "Is there anywhere on this ship you haven't gone? Captain Hollys gave me a tour of the gondola, but I couldn't tell you where the guardsroom is."

"Below and aft," Maggie said. "Just forward of the storage bay where the landaus are."

"Goodness." Claire slid a hand under Rosie's feet and carried her out into the corridor, closing the door behind them. "You sound like a proper airman."

"Only 'cos Willie laughed at me when I called the bow the front." She kept pace with Claire without effort. Regular meals, exercise, and hope were causing her to grow. Soon she would be past Claire's elbow and asking to have her skirts let down. "He's got nuffink to be proud of—a month ago he couldn't've said nor bow nor front."

"Wouldn't, Maggie. You know why."

"I know. Still. He oughtn't to've laughed and called me a silly gumpus."

They passed into the dining saloon and closed the door behind them. Ship's rule—doors left open tended to swing to and fro and smash walls and people when wind gusts affected their trim. At the sideboard were two little nightgown-clad figures, and a taller one with his nightshirt tucked into his pants. Willie turned at the sound of the door and a smile broke out that was brighter even than the moonglobe on the rail above the dishes of food.

"Lady! I saved you some trifle."

"You did not." Lizzie tolerated fibs in others about as often as she told them herself. "You'd 'ave eaten that quick enough if she 'adn't come in."

"You're too kind, Lord Wilberforce." As the son of an earl, Willie outranked her, even if he was only five. "But I must see to Rosie here first."

"You found 'er." Lizzie smiled at her twin. "I was that worried we wouldn't."

"She found her way to my cabin like the lady of resources she is," Claire said fondly, crumbling a blueberry scone into a Spode saucer and sprinkling a palmful of tiny red grapes on it. Rosie fell upon the food, and Claire filled a second saucer with water from a cut crystal carafe. "Now that I know she is traveling with us, I shall mention it to Mr. Skully. He will see that the crew knows she is one of our party and not a future meal."

Willie gasped. "No one will eat Rothie, will they? Papa will throw them overboard if they do."

His charming lisp was fading, only cropping up now in moments of stress. "It shall not come to that, my lord."

"My lord," Lizzie mimicked in her best private-school voice, and nudged Willie so hard in the ribs that the whipped cream wobbled on top of his trifle and the blackberry he'd so carefully placed at the summit rolled off onto the floor.

Rosie dispatched it with the speed of a striking cobra.

His face crumpled and Claire replaced the blackberry with another, and a second for Rosie, before the storm broke. "Rosie says thank you for the berry, your lordship," she said. "And for being a gentleman who always puts a lady before himself."

The skies cleared and Claire did not point out that he had already eaten half the trifle he had offered her. She cut a slice of apple pie instead, and poured cream over it.

Even now, she could not quite believe that the food would not disappear as magically as it came. As the daughter of a marquis, she had grown up eating mounds of food in multiple courses—so much that it regularly went back to the kitchen uneaten, to be made into something else or distributed to the poor. But in those dark days between being forced out of her home in Wilton Crescent and taking up residence in the river cottage in Vauxhall, she had gone hungry for days at a time. She had been reduced to foraging for the scraps that had once been thrown away, and she never forgot it.

She would never take food, shelter, and companionship for granted again.

The closing of the door signaled the arrival of yet another midnight marauder. Jake joined them and began piling cold meat and cheese on a thick slice of bread.

"Couldn't you sleep, Jake?" Claire cut a slice of beef into beak-sized bits, then put them in Rosie's saucer.

His gaze followed. "Found 'er, did you?"

Clearly she was the only one who had not been permitted knowledge of the stowaway. "She came along the piping to my cabin."

He nodded, mouth full. "Told 'em she'd come down when she got hungry. Bird's not stupid."

"She didn't feel safe," Maggie informed him. "I think she's clever for finding the Lady all her own self."

"Not feelin' so safe neither," Jake mumbled around the beef. "How much longer we goin' to be floatin' around under this big gasbag?"

"Why, Jake," Claire said in some surprise. "I thought you were enjoying your duties in the gondola with Captain Hollys."

"I'd enjoy 'em more if I couldn't see out." He began to build another sandwich. "Gondola's mostly glass held together with strips of brass an' curly bits of wood. Makes a fellow woozy."

"Hard to steer if you can't see out," Tigg observed.

Jake cuffed him on the shoulder, but since the sandwich was in that hand, it wasn't much of a blow. "I'd like to see you up there wi' the navigation charts an' nowt but stars and waves to go by."

"Not me," Tigg said, apparently unmoved. "I'm 'appy in the aft gondola, wi' little windows and big engines. Mr. Yau—he's the first engineer—he says I'm a dab hand wiv 'em."

"Hard to be a dab hand at anyfink after only three days." Jake wiped the crumbs off his face with his sleeve and eyed the pie.

"Jake, that weren't kind," Maggie said. "Who was it told me the captain let him take the rudder wheel for ten minutes? You got no call to talk to Tigg so, when from accounts he's as good as you."

"Three days is enough to show you everyfink you don't know." Jake cut the pie with the knife he kept at his belt, and wolfed it down without benefit of a plate.

"I don't know anything, that's wot I know," Tigg said bravely. "But I'm workin' on it, not complainin' about it."

When Jake stabbed the pie again, Claire opened her mouth to remonstrate about both greed and unkindness. But when he offered the second slice to Tigg, and the latter took it, she turned her attention to Rosie, whose appetite was finally satisfied. An apology had been given and accepted, and it was a foolish woman who would intrude on affairs of honor between gentlemen.

She hoped they would become gentlemen, in any event. Some day.

Even Jake.

For more, find *Magnificent Devices* at your favorite online retailer!

ABOUT THE AUTHOR

RITA Award® winning author and Christy finalist Shelley Adina wrote her first novel when she was 13. The literary publisher to whom it was sent rejected it, but he did say she knew how to tell a story. That was enough to keep her going through the rest of her adolescence, a career, a move to another country, a BA in Literature, an MFA in Writing Popular Fiction, and countless manuscript pages.

Shelley is the author of twenty-four novels published by Harlequin, Time/Warner, and Hachette Book Group, and several more published by Moonshell Books, Inc., her own independent press. She writes romance, paranormals, and the Magnificent Devices steampunk adventure series, and under the name Adina Senft, also writes women's fiction set in the Amish community.

Shelley is a world traveler who loves to imagine what might have been. Between books, she loves playing the piano and Celtic harp, making period costumes, quilting, and spoiling her flock of rescued chickens.

SHELLEY ADINA

Available now

The Magnificent Devices series:
Lady of Devices
Her Own Devices
Magnificent Devices
Brilliant Devices
A Lady of Resources
A Lady of Spirit
A Lady of Integrity
A Gentleman of Means
Devices Brightly Shining (Christmas novella)

Caught You Looking (Moonshell Bay #1)
Immortal Faith

The Glory Prep series
Glory Prep
The Fruit of My Lipstick
Be Strong and Curvaceous
Who Made You a Princess?
Tidings of Great Boys
The Chic Shall Inherit the Earth

COMING SOON

Fields of Air, Magnificent Devices #10
Fields of Iron, Magnificent Devices #11
Fields of Gold, Magnificent Devices #12

Caught You Listening, Moonshell Bay #2
Caught You Hiding, Moonshell Bay #3

Everlasting Chains, Immortal Faith #2
Twice Dead, Immortal Faith #3

Made in the USA
Middletown, DE
17 December 2015